Gilgath

And the Realm of the Drake

Book 1 of the "With us" Collection

John Thompson

Cover Art by John Thompson

Additional Art by John Thompson

www.BurkhartBooks.com

Bedford, Texas

Contents

Jn 3:17

Dear Reader:

The story you are about to read is meant for many. It's meant to soften and touch hearts, encourage healing, and shake your perspective. May it encourage revelation; may this book be a blessing to you. Also, even though a man wrote this story, he did not do it alone. I feel that The Holy Spirit guided me, holding my hand through the whole process. May the Lord bless you in reading this like he did me in writing it.

Love,
John

Warning:

The Content of this book is somewhat violent and a bit dark at times.

P.S. Please, give the _whole_ book a look.

Small Beginnings

On the quiet edge of the nation of Typhril, among the seas of wheat, there lived a family in a large yet humble cabin. For generations this family has worked the soil, raised livestock, and earned quite the name for themselves. See, this family once went by a different name, but after several generations of rather generous individuals, they were called the Bringers. For they would bring aid to any who needed it. This was the clan of the great Sarah Bringer, who brought many wagons of food to the stranded soldiers forced into hiding on the southern lines of the Dead Lands. She risked life and limb so those boys could eat. When the nation was locked in combat with the beast-men of the north, later called the Batille, Fargalo Bringer cooked piping hot meals for the garrison at Fort Hammer. When the fort was taken, he fought with knife and frying pan till his last breath. One survivor said Fargalo's pan put his mace to shame. He wielded that pan with the strength of a minotaur!

But none of these great men and women of the Bringer clan come close to Gilgath Bringer. When Gilgath was a young man around the age of 14, he lived with his father, Bregal, and mother, Mera, in the clan homestead. At this time, the nation had been consumed by darkness. The great dragon, Varcilyc, the dark drake from the south, seized power and the nation of Typhril was no more. Pyrodel had rose from its ashes. But something rather unexpected rose from the ashes as well.

"I ain't afraid of no dragon, or any of his drones!" Bregal shouted.

"You're daft to think this'll just all blow over! The reign of the drake will not pass us by! Me and mine are headed east!" shouted Bregal's brother Edio.

"Fine, good luck to ya! We'll be fine on our own!" yelled Bregal.

"Jaxi, Drellin! Is the wagon set?" called Edio. A boy and girl a little older than Gilgath slowly peaked in.

"Yes, papa," said the girl, "we're all ready."

"Good!" He turned back to Bregal. "If you think dad's coming back, he's not! Cut your losses and get away from this blight of a nation while there's still time!"

"I won't abandon our legacy, not unless I have no other choice," said Bregal.

"Then your line will die in this forsaken land! Goodbye Bregal, Mera, Gilgath, I hope the Provider protects you, but staying here is a death wish. It's just a matter of time," said Edio.

"It's a matter of time no matter where we go, Edio. You can't run from death, surviving isn't living," said Bregal.

"Maybe you're right, Breg, but I'll take my chances," Edio turned and stormed out of the cabin. The weight of the exchange stifled Gilgath's thoughts, then he snapped out of it and ran outside after his cousins.

"Wait! Please…" he called. Jaxi and Drellin were just sitting down in the wagon, they all looked up at him.

"Goodbye Gil, I'll miss you," said the Jaxi, tears streaming down her face.

"Farewell, Gil, good luck and all that," said the Drellin.

"Gil! Come here!" called his uncle Edio. Gilgath walked up to him, he could see in his uncle's eyes a great urgency… and pain. "Gil, I love you like you were my own, and I know you can't come with us, but someday… Someday you'll have to step out from behind your folk's shadow! You'll have to step up and be your own man!" Edio placed hand on Gilgath's shoulder, his tone dropped a whisper. "I'm afraid you'll have to a lot sooner than you think if'n you stay here. The countryside isn't safe, not anymore… Be prepared, son… Be strong." Edio quickly turned and snapped the reigns.

They then started their way down the windy road, leaving Gilgath standing alone in the dust. And with that, the clan was completely divided… forever. Edio led his family into the depths of the Eastern Wilderness. He'd rather risk living in the untamed forest than under an evil ruler. However, no one's heard from them since.

But life went on. The Bringers left behind still thrived at the clan's homestead, they went on about their day to day lives. Though there was always a lingering feeling of impending doom over their heads, they weren't directly effected by the reign of the dragon. They still drew comfort from their humble, sustainable lifestyle. Some hurt still lingered, but it was a very peaceful existence.

One day, Gil finally brought up the subject to his parents.

"Dad, where are cousin Drellin and Jaxi and uncle Edio gonna live?" Gilgath asked. "What will they do without fields, crops, or animals?" By now, Mera was fighting tears. Bregal was holding back his emotions.

"I must be strong for the boy," he said to himself.

"Well, son" Bregal started, "I don't know. Edio thinks that the Provider will care for him and his family. After all, your granddad Elkvich was a Keeper." He paused for a moment. "I really hope he's right, I really do."

"About the Provider taking care of Edio, or about what granddad would say about the Lamb?" Gilgath asked.

"Both … But mostly about the Lamb," said Bregal.

"Would you like to hear the story of the Lamb again, Gil?" Mera asked.

"Sure," Gilgath said, "I think I still remember most of it. The Keepers would have visions from the Provider that in Typhril's darkest hours, a being of great power would destroy the drake's reign forever!"

"Not this again!" Bregal interrupted.

"Oh hush, Breg! If you don't want to hear it, then you can go do something outside. Besides, dinner won't be done for a bit anyway." Along with this, Mera sent Bregal a stern look.

"I guess that's fine," Bregal said. "Just don't forget to call me in this time!"

"That only happened once!" she shouted. Her tone changed "But I promise I won't do that ever again, *my big, sweet, sensitive, man.*"

"Ok, ok, I love you too," and with that, he was out the door. Mera turned back towards her son.

"Where were we?" She asked.

"Umm, Typhril's darkest hour?" Gil said.

"Right," she got up and strode elegantly across the room to the kitchen area. The aroma of a hearty stew filled the fresh spring air as she stirred a pot on the pot-bellied stove. "This Being," she went on, "was thought to be in the form of a lamb, a clean, beautiful lamb. Your granddad would often quote the Living Book, "Only a Being of *true* love can herald the Provider's flock back into his arms. This Being will be humble in appearance, pure beyond measure, perform amazing feats, and be whiter than snow. The Lamb of the Provider shall thwart the darkness. Whoever believes in Him shall be made whole, and take their place in the never-ending dance of eternity." While the drake found this prophesy rather amusing, he still put a bounty on the heads of any convicted Keepers." At this she looked down, her face solemn. "Your granddad, Elkvich, was what held our family together for so long. He loved your father, me, your cousins, and you very much … He was jolly, wise and such a kind man. He's the one that taught us about the Provider, the Lamb, and many other truths."

"What, other truths, mom?" Gil asked.

"The drake," she looked up into her sons eyes. Anger was in her stare, "It took our nation out from under our very feet! It devours and corrupts all it touches! Typhril was once a mighty nation, now it's poison to the world!"

"Didn't Varcilyc changed our nation to Pyrodel?" asked Gil. His mother's eyes grew fiery, her face tense.

"Gilgath Bringer, don't you *EVER* speak that name in this house again!" She shouted. "Who told you that name anyway?" Gil stared at the ground for a moment.

"Granddad told me ...."

"I see," she said, "Well, I'm surprised you remember him at all. You were so young when he died."

"We don't even know *if* he died," Gil muttered.

"There's nothing wrong in hoping for the best, son," she said, "but your dad knows what he saw. And I'll trust you not to pry for details. It's still a painful subject, even for me." She turned and strode to the door. "DINNER TIME!" She bellowed out to all the countryside.

As evening came and went, so too did the day's nice, warm sun, a rather frigid dark had swept in in its place. Gil awoke in the middle of the night; he could hear the unease of their livestock. Gil stumbled out of bed and down the hall toward the main room. With his thoughts still fuzzy, he didn't think to wake his parents. But instead, Gil fumbled around near the doorway for the lantern, lit it, then grabbed his father's hatchet. He then proceeded to unblock the door and head out into the night. Once outside, he could feel the crisp coolness, see the revealing blue hue of the full moon, and hear the hundreds of crickets playing their song's in the distance. He looked to the barn and pens. The small herd was scrambling in one corner of the fence.

Glancing around, Gil saw no immediate threat, though they did seem to be avoiding the areas nearest the tree line. Not thinking much about it, Gil opened up the barn doors and let the animals in. They flooded in. In fact, one large cow almost knocked him over, while another stepped on his big toe.

"Eh! Ungrateful beef," he muttered.

Once all the sheep, cattle and etcetera were in, he shut and locked the doors. While sliding the latch, he felt a chilling sensation. It was as if someone or something was watching him. He whipped around holding the lantern out to the darkness. Several steps toward the tree line revealed a small white lamb hidden beneath the shadow of the trees. He looked at the little thing with intrigue. For this lamb, the smallest of the bunch, seemed quite calm. It even dared to go where the others were terrified to. Gil considered this for a moment and even admired its boldness.

"Hey there little one," he said calmly, "time to go to the barn." The lamb stared at him blankly as he slowly crept closer.

The Lamb turned its head to the thicket of the tree line; Gil did the same. There was suddenly movement in the brush. Gil raised the lantern in the direction of the noise, when a large wolf lept out and came sprinting right at him! With trembling hands, he raised the hatchet, and when the beast was close, buried it into the wolf's shoulder! The beast collided into him, sending both of them to the ground. With the lantern fallen and extinguished, Gil could barely make out the features of the injured beast that lay on top of him. He could feel the wet cold of its blood, though. The wolf stirred and slowly rose from him. Its figure emerged out of the shadow and into the moonlight where it stood like a man!

It reared its head back and released a blood chilling how; the howl was met and overpowered by a great guttural roar. A bright light lit the area. Gil turned to the light and saw a great golden lion where the lamb once stood. The lion lunged forward and pounced on the wolf, bringing it to the ground. The lion had its jaws around the wolf's throat; the wolf writhed and flailed before finally going limp. In a blink, the lion disappeared, and the lamb stood once more! Gil could hear his parents yelling and rushing past the barn to the tree line. Mera had a lantern, Bregal had a crossbow.

"Son, are you al-" Mera stopped."What on terra is that!"

"Looks like a wolf man," said Bregal. He knelt down next to Gil and looked him over. "Looks like it didn't get you though. That's good, but what got it?" Gil slowly turned and pointed at the lamb.

"That little lamb did *this*? Did you hit your head, son?" Asked Bregal.

"No–no sir, I seen it! When that wolf was on me, a big gold cat appeared and killed it! When the wolf died, it became a lamb again!" Gil paused for a moment, then he stood up. "Mom, dad, I think this might be *the* Lamb?"

"Maybe," said Bregal.

"You might be right, Gil," said Mera, "but what should we do?"

"Well," said Bregal, "let's put a collar on it and put it with the other sheep. We can figure something out in the morning."

As the sun dawned on the horizon, it painted the sky with pinks and yellows. The morning dew glistened in the early rays of the new day. A shallow ocean of mist hung over the fields and valleys. Gil awoke to his small room engulfed in a golden light. He sat up in his bed; still weary from his hard night's sleep. It was a few moments before he remembered what happened the previous night. He made his way across the room, down the hall, and to the main room. Mera was in the corner kitchen area whipping something up for breakfast. Bregal sat on a chair next to the stove sharpening several axes and hatchets.

"So, how'd you sleep?" Bregal asked. Mera jumped and turned.

"Yes, dear, how did you sleep?" Before Gil had a chance to answer, she had her arms wrapped around him in a great hug.

"I'm alright, mom, I slept fine," Gil said, struggling in her grasp.

"Are you sure? That was quite an ordeal! A traumatic event to say the least!" she insisted.

"Oh, Mera," said Bregal, "leave the boy alone. He's got enough to deal with without you smothering him to death."

"Keep off!" said Mera. "He may be a young man, but he's still our little boy!" her tone shifted. "Besides ... it's not every day you fight a creature of darkness."

"A what?" asked Gil.

"The wolf man," said Bregal, "he was a creature of darkness. Some of the boys down at the pub were talking about them one night. They say the drake blessed folks with dark powers ... powers of the unnatural sort. The wolf men they call Lycanthrope, and during the day, they look like normal people. See, it's the moon that seems to change them," he paused for a moment. "You're lucky to be alive, son."

"Now that's enough of that, Breg! You'll give him nightmares for sure talkin like that!" scolded Mera. Gil stayed silent, still in his mother's clutches.

"So," Gil started, "was that actually a real person?"

"He might of been at one point, but that was a beast that attacked you. You shouldn't feel guilty for defending yourself," said Bregal.

"That's right," said Mera, "even though you should have woke us up first! ... We're still proud of our brave young man. Besides, it was the Lamb that killed it!"

"Yeah, what about the Lamb?" asked Gil.

"Well," said Mera "your father and I were talking

about it and we thou-" She was interrupted by the faint but growing sound of several galloping horses.

Bregal laid aside his axe and whetstone, stepped across the room, and peered through the window to see what "guests" where headed their way.

"Two dark riders … looks like that Lycan had friends," Bregal said. "Mera, grab the crossbow and cover me through the window, I'll talk to them. Hopefully there'll be no need for violence," he turned to Gil. "But if there is, I'll need your help, son. I just sharpened this hatchet. Go ahead, you've earned it." He handed Gil the same hatchet he used the previous night, now clean and sharp. Bregal looked into his son's eyes.

"You've had to grow up a lot in the past couple days. You're growing to be a brave man, and I couldn't be more proud." With that, Bregal headed outside.

Mera manned one of the front windows, but was careful to stay in the shadows. Gil clutched his hatchet tightly. He recalled the last time he had to use it. He also remembered the blood, and how terrified he was. He feared what would happen to his father. Gil snapped out of it and stood listening, pressing himself against the door. The galloping grew louder, two riders cloaked in black trotted down the dirt road that wound through the fields and rolling hills. In a few short moments, they arrived at the homestead. Both rode dark horses, one rider was rather big and fat, the other was thin with a dark sharp beard and high cheek bones. Both adorned in black cloaks.

"Good morning!" called the thin one. "Is this the Bringer's residence?"

"Aye, it is," said Bregal.

"Then you must be Bregal. Your neighbors hold you in very high esteem. Though, I did picture the house being a bit larger … But since it's just the three of you anymore I'm sure it's more than enough room!" The thin rider paused for reply, but got none. "Right! Well, I suppose I'll get right to it then! We're wondering if you've seen our little brother."

"You two are the first to come down that road in a while," Bregal said.

"The thing is, he may not have used the road. You see, we're members of a rather unique or *gifted* group of individuals. Our pack won't rest until we are all accounted for," said the thin rider.

"Sorry, haven't seen anyone else around here for some time," Bregal said.

"That's a shame, because unlike the other farms we've visited, this place reeks of his stench. I say stench because somehow … you managed to kill him." At this, the thin rider dismounted his horse and strode up to Bregal face to face.

"So," said the thin man, "I'll ask you again. Have you seen our little brother?"

Bregal stared down at the thin man. While tension was building in the silence, the big rider slowly reached for his bow. Seeing this, Mera shot a bolt. It pierced clean through the big riders head. The thin man jerked around in surprise. Bregal then pulled out his knife and buried its hilt deep under the thin man's ribs.

"You won't be hunting any more families *ever* again," Bregal said. The thin man dropped to the ground writhing and coughing up blood. He eventually laid still. Gil opened the door and stepped out.

"You alright, dad?" asked Gil.

"Yeah, son, I'm fine. Good thing your mother's a better shot than I am." Mera stepped outside.

"What are we gonna do about this, Breg?"

"Well, honey, the way I see it, we could leave and try to find the Keepers, if there's any left. Or, we could stay and fight. Cause, there's no way we've seen the last of these *things*."

"Leave our home?" asked Mera.

"Where would we go?" asked Gil.

"Well, we'd take the Lamb to the Keepers. They'd know what to do with it," said Bregal.

"So we'd just give everything up and live on the road trying to find a group of righteous rebels that may not even still exist?" asked Mera.

"It's either that or wait till skinny and fatty's friends show up looking for them too," said Bregal.

"I guess you're right," said Mera. "When you put it that way, what choice do we really have?"

It took till the afternoon, but the Bringers loaded up their essentials, food, weapons, and other useful items (and let's not forget the Lamb). The three then mounted their two "new" black horses and set out to the nearest village.

"We'd better trade these horses when we get to town. Otherwise, we may get more trouble," said Bregal.

"And what about the farm? Who will tend the animals?" asked Mera.

"We could see if the Macgrooners would look after them," said Gil.

"Hey, now that's an idea! Their homestead's just around the next bend," said Bregal. "I'll go have a word with Ol' Seth and see if he'd be willing to send one of his boys out while we're gone … If they're still around."

When they came to a fork in the road, Bregal went on to the Macgrooner homestead while Mera, Gil and the Lamb stayed behind.

"Mom," said Gil. "Why are you so good with a bow?

I thought dad did most of the hunting."

"Oh," she started, "there's a lot you don't know about your old mom and dad."

"Like what?" Gil asked hesitantly.

"Well, for starters, I'm a foreigner."

"Pft, I knew that," he said.

"Really? Well, mister know–everything, do you know *where* I'm from?" she asked.

"A Mid–Terra country?" Gil said.

"I'm from the Mid-Terra Island of Makorru. My dark skin and elegant figure are a dead give-away. I was a mighty warrior who's heart fell captive to a big, strong, handsome, and not to mention hairy man from across the Mid-Terra Ocean."

"Alright, mom, I get it." Gil said. Mera gazed longingly into the horizon. The Lamb stared off toward the Macgrooners, and gave a little puff in that direction, but Mera and Gil didn't notice.

"What a man he was … Oh!- and is! We married in Makorru and came back here to the Bringer clan homestead."

"What was dad doing in Makorru?"

"Well, our nation was going through some tough times. With the rise of the drake, the new nation of Pyrodel wasn't interested in trading with the Mid–Terra Islands anymore. He'd rather let us starve, then swoop in and take control with his enchanted followers. As skilled as the Makorru are at archery and trapping, they wouldn't stand much chance against such powerful evil."

"So, you and dad ran away before things got bad?"

"No," her tone changed, now solemn and distant. "Your father and cousins lead a convoy to bring food to the islands, but the drake got word. They weren't at our island for more than a few weeks when the Dark Hand showed up."

"I've never heard of them before," he said.

"I know … this memory is painful for us. The Dark Hand was a small group of powerful priestesses. There were six in total. They killed many Makorru warriors, several of your cousins, and your granddad," she said.

"Elkvich?" Gil asked.

"No, Whantero. Your father tried to save both me and my father, but couldn't carry us both to safety. My father was moved by Bregal's courage and honor. With his last breath, he gave your father his blessing and signet amulet as proof. After a mighty battle, and with some aid from a couple other tribes, the priestesses eventually retreated back to the mainland. Only four of those witches survived. That day, we celebrated a victory, mourned your grandad, and had a wedding."

"What a day …" Gil commented. Mera stared blankly nodding her head.

"Yes, what a day … Don't bring this up to your father. He-" she paused and looked out to the road. Bregal was returning in the distance. She turned back to Gil. "Next time we can talk about how your father learned the ways of the axe. He's a champion thrower, ya know!"

Bregal slowed his horse to a stop once back to the fork. Mera stared at him with an admiring grin.

"Looks like you two had a good conversation," Bregal said.

"They're always the best whenever *you're* not around," she said, still smiling.

"What's that look for?" Bregal asked.

"I just love you is all," she said.

"Oh, well, I love you too. Anyway … it's all taken care of with the Macgrooners. They're willing to lend a hand given the circumstances. And, if we hurry, we might be able to make it to Herrontown before sunset."

"All the way to Herrontown?" said Mera. "There's no way!"

"Not with an attitude like that, my dear," Bregal retorted.

"If we ride fast we might," chimed Gil.

"That's the spirit, son!" said Bregal.

And with that, the party set out. They trotted down the winding road, over hills, around ponds and lakes, over a bridge or two and into the tall, deep green of Iron Oak Forest.

Herrontown

"Breg!" called Mera. "I don't like this! It's getting dark and there's no sign of town."

"It's coming up soon," he said. "How's our little traveler doing?"

"I'm fine, dad," Gil said trying not to giggle.

"Gil, it's too much to have to deal with your antics right now!" barked Bregal. "Now, how is the Lamb!"

"Fine, I guess. It hasn't moved much since we started. Maybe it got sick from the motion of the horse. I doubt it's used to riding on the back of some other animal."

"We should stop and rest soon," said Mera.
"I told you, we're almost there," said Bregal. "We'll find an inn and we can all get some good rest. Tomorrow we can check our supplies and look at any shops nearby."

They traveled on through the winding road deeper and deeper into the long dark that is the forest. The crescent moon rose as twilight turned to night sky. The night air was filled with the symphony of the nocturnal wildlife. This continued for several hours. Then, finally, they could see the flickering light of a torch. Once closer, it was revealed to be a lamppost. A trail of them lead along the road till it reached the village. As they progressed, the dirt of the road soon became cobble. When they grew near to the town, they could see the busy nightlife bustling about the town square. It was as if a small festival was being held. Many vendors of food, drink and wears serviced the masses as children ran about playing and laughing.

"See," said Bregal, "I told you!" Mera shot him a skeptical look. "Now we don't have time to join the festivities," Bregal went on. "We must find an inn without drawing too much attention."

They dismounted and walked on through. As they strode, a shop-keep on the edge of the festival called out to them.

"Happy Leaving day! And my, that's quite the hatchet you have there, sir!" said a short stalky man. Actually, he was just over half the height of a normal sized man. His red beard almost touched the ground, and his pleasant cheekbones gave him a most jolly demeanor. His eyes drifted toward the Lamb where he stared for a moment.

"Oh this?" replied Bregal. "I won it in a competition."

"Really!" The short man jumped a bit. "See, I'm the town smithy. *I* am Rolldrin." He then proceeded to bow.

Mera stepped forward. "It's nice to meet you, Rolldrin. I'm Mera, this is my husband, Bregal, and this is our son, Gil!"

"Welcome, to Herrontown! You've caught us during our fall festival." Rolldrin's tone shifted. "Now about that axe, you *won* it? From who?"

"Well, it was a few years ago," said Bregal, "I believe it was during the winter celebration in Hallowburg. Why?"

"I believe I recognize the craftsmanship. May I see it?" Bregal handed the hatchet to the short man. Rolldrin gently took it and looked it over with care. After a moment, he handed it back.

"It's one of mine alright. I gave it to one of the lads in these parts when he became a man. He set out into the world to find his own way. I wonder how it ended up in Hallowburg? I'll be sure to inform his parents; they haven't heard or seen him for some time. Looks like you've taken good care of it though! Thank you," he paused for a moment. "Well, while you're here, would you like to see all I have for sale?" His mood sprang right back up to jolly.

"Actually, we-," Mera was cut short.

"Sure we would!" said Bregal, Mera was now wearing the scowl.

"Well, come on in!" said Rolldrin. Bregal followed him into the shop.

"You might as well go with him," said Mera to Gil. "I'll find something to eat."

Gil followed his father inside. Rolldrin's shop was cozy and warm, the smell of a dead fire lingered in the air. Rolldrin soon lit a few lantern's revealing the armory which covered the walls, a plethora of arms and armor. Blades glinted, hilts twinkled, and shields shimmered in the dwindling light.

"What kind of weapons are we lookin' for? Or perhaps some armor?" asked Rolldrin. Bregal thought for a moment.

"Well, we'll need to travel light. So, probably not so much the armor, we could probably use some weapons though."

"Of course!" said Rolldrin. "Where're you all headed?"

"Well," said Bregal, "we're actually seeking the Keepers. We don't really have any idea where they are, but I'd imagine they're further toward the castle." Rolldrin's expressions grew serious again.

"You must be careful of whom you mention that too." He looked down for a moment. "Last I heard, there were a few skirmishes with them toward Granvult Mountain. The town Bejavia isn't too far from there, maybe one of the townsfolk will be of help."

"Who were they fighting?" asked Gil.

"The Keepers were helping the town. Word got out of their arrival, and shortly after leaving, the head priestess caught them."

"Did they escape?" asked Gil.

"Not sure, no one's heard from that area for months," said Rolldrin. "If you're seeking the Keepers, I'll help you, but not completely for free. I still have a business to run after all."

"You believe in their cause?" asked Bregal.

"How could I not?" asked Rolldrin. "My people owe a lot to the Keepers. They helped my kin keep the Trollian at bay."

"Trollian, so you're a dwarf?" asked Bregal.

"Yes, sir, I'm from the Red Valley to the south."

"Wow!" said Gil. "But that's so far away! Beyond the Dead Lands …"

"Aye, but not far enough, the drake took our home too. Although to take the Red Valley, he used most his forces. I heard that afterwards, he took to the north. I guess after having little success at the great south wall that dark spawn decided to take matters into his own hands."

"Right," said Bregal, "we won all the assaults from the drakes."

"Except the one that counted most!" said Rolldrin.

"Granddad Elkvich used to sa-," Gil was cut short.

"Elkvich!" exclaimed Rolldrin. "Elkvich Bringer? He's your Granddad?"

"And *my* father" said Bregal. Rolldrin jumped back to jolly again.

"He saved my life during the Trollian war! There were few who survived the drake assault though, any who did ran or hid. But seeing you're Bringers, that changes things!" Rolldrin hustled over to a large chest and started rummaging through it.

"What weapons are we looking for?" he shouted over his shoulder.

"I have an axe or two already," started Bregal, "but maybe a sword for the boy, and a bow for the wife?"

After a few more moments of digging around, Rolldrin pulled out a slender sword with a long straight blade and brass hilt and pommel.

"I think this'll due for ya, lad!" said Rolldrin, handing it to Gil. Soon he pulled out a bow; it was short and lightweight with a quiver of arrows to match.

"That'll due for the lady," he said, handing it to Bregal. He then turned around with something else—two large yet slender kite shields. They came to two sharp points and the handles were positioned to take advantage of it.

"Now!" Rolldrin started. "That sword is made from some of the finest ingots in the Red Valley. It has a lot of platynite in it making it very light yet very strong. The bow and arrows are also reinforced with platynite; it has much power for such a small size, and the arrows are more durable than most. Those kite bracers are called the Claws of the Valley. They offer good offense, and a great defense. You're built like a brawler, Bregal; the Claws of the Valley will serve and protect you and your family well," Rolldrin said. Gil looked up at Bregal hesitantly.

"Can I tell him, dad?"

"After all this, I believe so," Bregal said. Rolldrin's expression became worrisome.

"Is something wrong? You don't like them?"

"I couldn't have asked for better," said Bregal.

"It's just that …" Gil started. "We believe we've found the Lamb."

"Really?" asked Rolldrin. "The little thing you were riding with? How can you be sure?"

"It killed a Lycanthrope," said Bregal. Rolldrin took a step back and stared at the ground in bewilderment.

"My, my …" he said, "To think I should live to see *the* Lamb. Well, go ahead and take the weapons as a gift to your cause. Is there any more I can do to help?" Bregal smiled.

"No, no, you've done more than enough, we thank you. Could you point us toward the inn though?" Bregal asked.

Rolldrin directed them, then Bregal and Gil headed out the door. When they emerged, they looked around for Mera. They found her across the street sitting on a small wagon bound to a large brown horse. As they got closer her sweet smile soon changed to a bitter scowl.

"Bregal Bringer! How much did all this cost?" she demanded.

"Not one cent," he retorted. "And what about you? How much did all *this* cost?"

"Not one cent," she said smugly.

"Well, I guess we both did pretty good then," Bregal said.

"I guess so," said Mera, slowly breaking into a smile. And with that, they headed over to the inn.

Later that night, while they were all asleep, the Lamb stirred. It walked over to their heap of weapons laying on the floor. Gil wearily awoke at the sound of its movement. "What's it doing?" he thought. The Lamb then opened its mouth and breathed a golden dust on their weapons. Still groggy, and now confused, after a brief moment, Gil drifted back to sleep.

The next morning, Mera awoke earliest. She took into account their provisions, then headed to the marketplace to visit the local grocer. After buying some food for the road, she made her way back to the inn, a small commotion was stirring at the town entrance, a large man cloaked in black was hassling one of the townsfolk. She started toward the ruckus, determined to put an end to it. Then she recognized the cloaked man's horse, her heart sank.

"If he finds that tradesman, he'll know what we look like, what we're riding and soon, where we've been in town," she thought to herself. "It's time to leave. I wouldn't want anyone to get hurt on our account." As soon as she got back to the inn, she woke up Bregal and Gil.

"Wake up!" she shouted. "We need to leave now!"

"What? Why?" asked Bregal, still half asleep in bed.

"Another Lycanthrope just came to town, and he's looking for us!" she said.

"If it comes to it, we'll just kill him like the others …" said Bregal.

"Bregal Bringer! You will not endanger the lives of your family or the town just so you can get an extra hour or two of sleep!"

With that, she stomped over to his bed and plopped down on his stomach. When that had no effect, she began to bounce.

"Alright, alright, woman!" he said, "I'm awake! You can get off me now!"

After they finished dressing, they loaded up and headed out once again on the winding road through the dark of Iron Oak Forest. The chill of morning still lingered as the sun slowly peaked over the horizon heralding warmth and light to yet another new day. The wagon glided as the large brown horse trotted down the now dirt road. They soon passed the last lamppost. After about an hour or two, Bregal brought the horse down to a slow walk.

"Why are you slowing down, Breg?" asked Mera.

"We got a long way to go. I know she's big and strong, but even Meredith here has her limits," said Bregal.

"You named her Meredith?" asked Gil.

"Yeah, what of it?" asked Bregal.

"Really?" asked Mera.

"What's wrong with Meredith?" asked Bregal.

"Oh, nothing," said Mera, "except she already has a name. Her name is Walnut."

"I like Meredith," said Bregal, "It's wild and beautiful." There was silence for a moment.

"She's a horse, Breg," said Mera, "she's a horse that pulls a wagon. That's probably one of the least wild things there is!"

"Well fine, Mera," said Bregal, "You all like the name Walnut better?"

"Kinda," said Gil.

"Yes, it's cute and ironic," said Mera.

"Well, fine! It doesn't really matter anyway. I don't under-," Bregal was cut short by a sudden large raindrop. He looked up at the sky to see an ocean of dark clouds looming overhead. Fat droplets of water started to sprinkle down. "This storm looks like it's gonna get real bad real quick," he said. "I think I see a cave at the base of that mountain up ahead. We can rest there till the storm's over."

Just off the road, there was a large mouthed cave that could house them all. Bregal entered first, carefully inspecting the ground for any sign of residency.

"All clear!" he yelled out to the others.

They left the cart and Walnut in the tree line to escape the now growing storm. The family unrolled their knapsacks and any covers they had brought and slowly drifted to a rough and very uncomfortable night of sleep. The wind picked up as a parade of thunder and lightning marched its way through the sky. At one point, during the cold of the night, Gil started to shiver and briefly woke from his sleep. He pulled his covers tighter and tossed about on the ground for a moment. Shortly after settling, something warm and fuzzy snuggled in next to him. His shivering soon ceased and he began to drift back to sleep again.

Gil jumped as something woke him with a loud "Splat!" He looked around for the cause of the noise, Mera and Bregal woke up too and met his gaze. Their eyes soon led outside. The forest still dripped with fresh rain, and the mud was still soft, the sky still shrouded by a veil of clouds, but the rain had stopped. The dreary grey of an overcast morning hung over the forest. They soon spotted something laying in the mud at the mouth of the cave. Bregal cautiously made his way over to investigate.

"It's a man, looks like he's dead!" called Bregal.

He slowly started to look up, then immediately leapt back inside the cave. As he did, dozens of bodies hailed down from the sky! Men and women, young and old, all laid lifeless in the mud. Mera let out a gasp and held Gil tight against her bosom.

"Don't look, dear," she whispered.

A loud roar echoed over the forest as the drake flew overhead and into the distance. Bregal slowly stepped to the mouth of the cave again.

"So that's what the devil looks like," he muttered.

The Lamb walked up to one of the corpses and nudged it a couple times with its snout. It paused for a moment, then looked at the others.

"Did the drake cause this?" asked Gil.

"He's a master manipulator, son," said Bregal, "He must of convinced these poor people it'd be worth it," Bregal paused and stared down at one of the bodies, a young man not much older than Gil. "I can't imagine what kind of lies and torment could cause this kind of suicide... and I don't want to."

Gil turned and made eye contact with the Lamb. Several small droplets of water trickled down the sides of its face. "Hadn't it-," he thought to himself, "hadn't it stopped raining?"

Bejavia

After a few moments of gathering their belongings, and their wits, they loaded up and headed out once more. It wasn't long though before they reached the next town. This place was much different from the warm cheeriness of Herrontown. The streets were deserted, bits of charred wreckage littered the town, partially burned homes and shops were the only buildings left. Some of them were nothing more than piles of ash. All was silent, no birds chirping or townspeople bustling. Once they reached the village square, they saw a large stone slab. It was coated in a deep crimson liquid and several knives sat at its corners.

"Breg …" said Mera, "I don't like this."

"Neither do I," said Bregal. "Let's keep moving.

Hopefully we won't attract any attention. Keep your weapons ready, though."

The wagon slowly made its way across the square. Once almost across, Gil saw someone standing off to the side of them. Soon there were more on all the other sides too.

"Mom …" Gil whispered.

"I know, dear," she said.

The wagon was circled and completely cut off. The mob was full of unfriendly faces, and the sound of their inaudible murmuring could be heard. The wagon came to a stop. The crowd opened behind them revealing a dark cloaked figure. The Bringers, with weapons in hand, faced the new threat.

"Good morning!" called Bregal. "That was quite the storm last night, you folks al-"

"Silence!" said the figure, it was a woman's voice. "What do you think you're doing here?"

"Just passing through," said Mera.

"You will do no such thing! You are trespassing on sacrificial grounds! You will be held till Lord Varcilyc returns!" called the cloaked woman.

"And if we refuse?" asked Bregal. The woman laughed.

"*Refuse?* You have no choice! You will bear sacrifice one way or another or die!"

"I think I'll just take *you* on instead," said Bregal.

"You dare challenge a dragon priestess!" her tone grew fiery.

"Any day of the week, you wretched hag!" yelled Bregal.

She screamed with anger and sprinted at them. Her outstretched hands became covered with dark fire. Bregal lunged forward to meet her. Once she was fairly close, she stopped and thrust her hands at Bregal. He brought both his shields together and braced for the impact. A bright gold light on the shields met the deep flame. The fire scattered to the air and dissipated. Not a spark got past Bregal's shields. After a moment, the priestess let up on her flame. She was amazed and taken aback, for Bregal was untouched! Bregal chuckled a bit.

"You'll have to do better than that!" he said.

"How coul-" her words fell short as an arrow sunk into her heart. She fell lifeless to the ground. Bregal turned back to his wife.

"No sense in letting her have another go at you, dear!" Mera said.

The crowd started to stir with the sound of many swords being drawn. Bregal stepped back ready to defend his family from the infringing horde. Once closer, Gil could see something strange in the eyes of the townsfolk. There were no pupils, no color, just black. They drew very close when a mighty roar erupted from behind the small family. A deep roar, one that'd make your very soul quiver. The Bringers turned back around to the cart. Where the Lamb once lay, now stood a great, gold lion. Gil turned back to the crowd. Their eyes had color once more! The townsfolk stood dazed and confused.

"It did it!" Gil said. "It broke the dragon's cur-" he turned back to the cart only to find the Lamb again.

"It sure did, son," said Bregal. He patted the Lamb on the head. "Thank you," he said to it. One of the townsfolk approached them.

"I'm sorry for any trouble," said the man. He was middle aged, rather stalky in build, and had a long thick mustache.

"That dragon possessed us! He said … If we submitted, he'd spare the rest of the town," the stout man paused and looked around. He soon turned from confused to panicked.

"Where are the rest of them? Where are the women and children and elderly? Where is my wife and daughter?"

"I'm sorry," said Mera with tears starting to well up.

"A mixed lot found their way off the edge of the mountain this morning," said Bregal. "It was quick, but it looked like suicide," he said. The stout man kneeled to the ground.

"My Roseline would never do such a thing … would she?" he looked up at them.

"The drake himself was there, whispering lies to them … I'm sorry," said Bregal.

"And the children?" asked another man from the crowd. Bregal looked down. Mera was now in tears. Gil looked at the men, then pointed at the priestess and the stone altar. Many more men fell to the ground, most were crying for their lost loved ones. The stout man looked up at Bregal, tears streaming down his face.

"It would have been better for you to have let me die! It would have been better if we had died!" His expression changed to anger. "Why? Why didn't you kill us? Why didn't you kill us before we knew?" Bregal didn't answer. "They didn't do anything to deserve this! *We* didn't do anything to deserve this! All because the Keepers helped us out for a couple days? They brought this upon us!" On hearing this, Gil's temper flared. He marched over to stout man, still kneeling in the mud, and kicked him upside the jaw!

"Gil!" shouted Mera.

"How dare you blame the Keepers!" shouted Gil. The stout man was now laying on his back in shock. "Do you know what happened to those Keepers who helped you? That witch caught them and killed them!

Helping you cost them their lives! So don't you *dare* pin this calamity on them! This is the work of that dragon. He whispered lies to your loved ones, he's the one who used your children for his dark rituals. It wasn't the Keeper's, the Provider's … and it wasn't your fault either … I know I'm young, and you have more than enough to grieve over, but you're still alive! That's something, isn't it?" he paused and turned to the Lamb. "It wasn't us who saved you, it was the Lamb." The crowd's sobbing paused, the stout man got to his knees again and he stared down at the ground. His thoughts were suddenly interrupted by a small tongue licking his face. He opened his eyes to see the Lamb standing in front of him. The stout man hugged the Lamb and started weeping again.

Later, the Bringers headed back out on the road. The heartbroken men of the town grieved together and, thanks to the Bringers, and the Lamb, decided to set out from their town and try to find the Keepers as well. The men would meet up with the Bringers in about a week at the inn of Ember City.

The Bringers traveled for hours in silence. Each was caught up in processing the events of the day. So much had happened in such a short time, it wasn't even evening and yet they were already exhausted. Bregal turned over his shoulder to face his family.

"Son," he said.

"Yeah, dad?" asked Gil.

"About what you told those men … a bit course, don't you think?" asked Bregal. Gil turned his head toward the ground. "I thought we were gonna be in hot water again when you kicked that poor man flat on his back!" he paused for a moment. "But it must have been what they needed to hear. You gave them a reason to move on, a reason to live. Instead of getting lost in their own sorrow, they're doing something about it." Mera smiled and placed a hand on Gil's shoulder.

"Son," Bregal went on, "I know you're quiet in nature, but you helped set those men back on the right path. That's something you'll have to learn in life, every action or idle you take in any situation has repercussions. Every choice you make will determine the kind of man you grow into. And today, though risky, and hasty, you made, what turned out to be, a good choice. One that affected those men in a way you'll never know."

"That's right, dear," said Mera. "They now not only have something to fight for, but hope in. As long as there's hope, there's a reason to live," she said. Gil stared into the loving eyes of his parents.

"I've never lost my temper like that before," he said.

"It's alright to get angry sometimes," said Mera. "Just as it's alright to be sad or happy. The Provider gave us these things so we could feel what is right and what is wrong."

"It makes me think of something your granddad used to say," said Bregal. "Do you know why life is beautiful? Because it's fragile and fleeting. It takes so much to create and cultivate, but in an instant, it's gone," Bregal turned back around. "I'm proud of you, son. You'll be a great man someday."

"You'll make a great husband too!" said Mera. She smiled a bit brighter and gave Gil's chin a wiggly pinch. "Oh, you're such a handsome lad, I think you got the best parts of both of us! If we were in Makorru still, you'd already have a wife and maybe child on the way!" Gil's face turned red and he brushed his mother's hand away.

"A child? Already?" he asked.

"Well, sure!" said Mera. "As soon as the boys start to take a liking to the girls, they're old enough to wed! At least in my country…" she paused and jerked up suddenly. "Gil, have you started fancying girls yet?"

"For terra's sake, woman!" said Bregal. "After what we've been through today, you have the nerve to ask him about his personal manhood?"

"Why not?" she asked. "It'll help get his mind off the unpleasant. Well, Gil? Have ya?" Gil turned to the ground again.

"I don't really get to see many except when we're in town, but most of them are pretty."

"Any of them get you stirring?" Mera asked.

"Mera!" shouted Bregal.

"Well … maybe a little here and there" said Gil.

"See, Breg," said Mera, "he's already practically a man. I saw his whiskers startin' to come in and figured it's about time." She leaned over and swatted Bregal on the back. "We'll keep an eye out for a good one along the way, right, Breg?" Bregal muttered something under his breath.

"I think we have more pressing matters, but I'll keep an eye out …"

"A real good one too!" she insisted.

"Yes, dear," Bregal said.

"Good wife material!" said Mera.

"Of course …" muttered Bregal.

Gil was glad no one else was around but them. Although, it did lighten the mood for the rest of the evening. As night started to fall, the Bringers set up camp just off the road. The veil of clouds still hung overhead. The forest was engulfed by the vast dark of a starless night.

Gil tossed and turned in his sleep. His dreams were filled with the sight of the masses of townsfolk who had fallen to their deaths. He saw their faces, then the face of the drake. Gil was consumed with fear. He ran from the dragon's fire, but could not escape. Then, the fire turned into the black riders, who then turned into wolves. He then saw the priestess; she strode towards him, her fingers dripping with blood. She pulled out a large bloodied knife. Then suddenly, something changed. He drew his sword; it started to glow brightly, an endless beam of light stimmed from it. Gil found his courage; he swung the blade in the darkness, all the creatures disappeared when the light touched them. Gil felt peace throughout; he soon woke in the early morning. Looking over, he saw his parents still asleep, then he looked down at his bedding. The Lamb had come to comfort him once again.

The fresh dew of morning had settled on the forest. Streaks of morning light beamed through the leaves, limbs and needles of all sorts. The clouds had left, for now, and a bright new day was dawning the horizon. Mera prepared a fire and started cooking breakfast. Bregal packed and loaded anything not in immediate use. Gil huddled with the Lamb next to the fire. The crisp cool of morning was soon interrupted by the smell of a hot, well-cooked breakfast. The Bringers sat down and enjoyed a warm brief moment of calm, joy, and, for just a little bit, forgot all the troubles of the world.

"We should arrive at Gettlesburg by this evening," said Bregal.

"That's what you said about Herrontown!" said Mera.

"Well, we *did* arrive that same night, at least," said Gil.

"Thank you, son," Bregal then turned to Mera. "It was still a part of the same day, even if it was the end of it!" he smiled playfully.

"True, but I don't like being on the road in the dead of night. It's not smart, and it's not safe! We've been lucky so far, but you never know what's waiting just off the beaten path," said Mera.

"That sounds like something dad would say," chimed Gil.

"I know it," said Mera, "after spendin' so many years together, you start to rub off on one another."

"I'm sure we can handle anything that comes our way," said Bregal.

"I don't want to push it, dear," said Mera.

"Why not?" Bregal said. "With these new weapons of ours, not even a dragon priestess stands a chance!"

"It's not just the weapons …" said Gil.

"What do ya mean?" asked Bregal.

"Well, the other night, at the inn, I woke up to see the Lamb breathing a sort of gold dust on our weapons," said Gil

"Why didn't you say something, dear?" asked Mera.

"Well, I wasn't sure if it was a dream or not. I was still partially asleep," said Gil.

"Huh," said Bregal, "and here I thought old Rolldrin back in Herrontown was the best blacksmith in the world!"

"He still may be," said Mera, "that arrow I shot almost bore clean through! That's rare in a short bow of this stature." All was silent for a moment.

"I sold the animals," said Bregal.

"What!" said Mera.

"I sold the animals to old man Macgrooner," he said.

"But why, Breg?" asked Mera.

"Because I really wasn't sure if we'd make it back or not, and I figured we needed the money for the trip. I couldn't bring myself to sell the clan homestead, though … So, there'll be a home waiting for us, but … not much else …" All was silent again.

"Do you really think we might not make it back?" Gil finally asked.

"Only the Provider knows, son," said Bregal.

Eventually, the Bringers headed out down the road again. With a slight hint of gloom looming over them, they trudged forward to whatever lies ahead. Mera and Gil sat silently in the back of the wagon. Gil noticed a couple tears streaming down his mother's cheek. He slowly shuffled over and held her. She hugged him back and let a few more tears out. The Lamb slowly made its way over to them and laid across their laps. Mera stroked its beautiful, soft wool as she quietly sobbed. Gil let some tears out too. Eventually, Gil fell asleep, a deep sleep, the kind of sleep you can only get while safely in the arms of a parent or loved one. No nightmares this time.

Desolation

"Wake up, dear!" said Mera, as she shook Gil awake. "We need you to wake up!" her tone was soft but somewhat urgent.

"What's going on-" Gil paused as his groggy eyes peered around. They had entered a section of the forest that'd burned down. A wide expanse of charred emptiness surrounded them. But there was more than just the char of stumps and branches, there were lumps and heaps of something else in and on the char and ash.

"What *is* all this?" asked Gil.

"Not sure," said Bregal, "looks like a nasty fire made its way through. No sign of Gettlesburg, though."

"What are all those little lumps all over the place?" asked Mera.

"Ol' Orble at the pub used to tell all kinds of wild stories, one of them was about the trees in the depths of the forest."

"What about them?" asked Gil.

"Well, it turns out the Iron Oak Forest isn't just a name. There's a certain type of tree in the middle of the forest that has veins of iron at its core," said Bregal.

"An actual Iron Oak?" asked Mera.

"Yeah, I guess it's pretty valuable if harvested and refined correctly. It's supposed to be pretty hard stuff, and most people never venture that far into the forest to fetch it, so it's pretty rare," said Bregal.

"What's wrong with this part of the forest?" asked Mera.

"Well," he went on, "people have all sorts of strange stories. Like the presence of an odd race of hedgehog people, large viper-like worms, or great ground dragons called *salamanders*."

"Really, ground dragons?" asked Gil.

"They're just rumors, dear," said Mera.

"Still," said Bregal, "we should keep an eye out for anything of the sort."

The cart continued slowly and quietly along the path which slithered through the burnt and molten waste. After a while, Gil started to notice something moving in the soot behind them. He quietly got Mera's attention and pointed to the object slithering around.

"Weapons ready, dear," Mera said.

Bregal stopped the wagon. They all hopped out, ready for whatever new challenge awaited them. The burrowing creature soon emerged. A large bipedal lizard sprang up from the ground; it gurgled as it looked around seeming rather surprised.

"Wait!" someone screamed in the distance.

The Bringers all turned to one side of the road. A round stalky figure hobbled its way toward them. Once closer, they saw it was actually very hedgehog-like in appearance. It wobbled as it moved through the soot.

"Sal! What are ya doin' buggin' these nice folks for!" it continued. Its voice was rather scraggly, but sounded female. "You're lucky they didn't put a sword to your wrinkled throat, you old fool!"

The creature she called Sal turned to her and made a few gargling sounds.

"That's what you get for not paying attention!" The hedgehog woman turned toward the Bringer family. Gil could see all the jewelry and trinkets that hung and dangled this way and that from her long quills.

"I'm very sorry, dear ones, there's no need for alarm. He tends to get lost in his ventures, he's very old, ya see," Sal made a few more gurgles almost protestingly. "Oh, just shut it! You *are* old, and so am I!" she scolded. "Now, the least we can do is invite you for some tea for giving you such a fright."

"Oh, uh, noth-," Bregal started.

"That sounds lovely!" said Mera, smiling smugly at Bregal. He met her gaze with one of concern, to which she responded by gently squeezing his arm.

"Yes," said Bregal, "that'll be fine."

"Wonderful!" said the hedgehog woman. "Come this way!" she stopped mid step for a moment. "I'm so sorry," she started, "I've forgotten to introduce us. I am Spindley-quill Salamander, and this gargling bag of scales is my husband, Salderith Salamander."

Salderith's demeanor changed to one rather dignified, he even performed a small bow. The Bringers holstered their weapons and led the horse and wagon through the ash. Every few moments or so Spindley would say something over her shoulder like, "I hope you like nettle tea and flaggy biscuits," or, "I hope you're not too tired for tea," and of course, "lovely weather today, isn't it?" After a few more moments of this, Spindley stopped and turned to the Bringers.

"I'm so sorry, dears, I got so excited, I forgot to ask all *your* names," Spindley said.

"Oh," started Bregal. "I'm Gran-"

"He's Bregal!" interrupted Mera. Bregal sent her an annoyed leer, which she met with a kind smile. "I'm Mera, his wife," she went on, "and this is our son, Gil."

Spindley flashed a rosy smile and said, "It's nice to meet you all!" she then continued on as if nothing had happened.

They followed the two until they came to a small cottage just past the untouched tree line. Spindley went ahead and opened the door for them; the Bringers paused hesitantly for a moment.

"Well, come on in!" said Spindley. She soon read their hesitation. "Don't worry, it's much larger on the inside."

And it was; the cozy little room that was the cottage was just a front, a mud room of sorts. A place to take off any dirty boots and hang any gear; a stairwell lead down into the depths of the house. The narrow stairs soon turned into a spiraling staircase which lead further down into a great open expanse, a large, tall pocket of a tunnel. It was engulfed by the warm, flickering glow of over a dozen candles, and stained with the smells of the many meals of its past. It was a great, underground dining hall, with a large kitchen pocket to the side. Spindley and Salderith politely stood to one side.

"Go ahead and take a seat anywhere you'd like," said Spindley. "We'll have something for you soon enough."

The Bringers found a seat at the grand table. It was a table of Iron oak! It was so intricate and natural looking, it was as if the living wood was molded into table and chairs. After sitting down, suddenly it hit Gil.

"Mom!" he whispered to Mera. "I think we forgot the Lamb outside!" her eyes widened at hearing this.

"Best go get it, quickly!" she said.

Gil headed back up the stairs, the embarrassment of the situation started to set in a bit. They'd been so overtaken by the thought of a hot meal in comfort, they'd forgotten their most important member! Gil found his way up the winding staircase and out the cottage door. Once outside, he found the Lamb standing quietly next to the wagon. He wasn't more than a few steps from the doorway when an explosion erupted behind him! A large plank from the door struck him in the back of the head. Gil fell to the ground stunned and unsure of what had happened.

When Gil openned his eyes, he saw the cottage was nothing but a smoldering crater. All his scrambling thoughts, were interrupted by the sound of large footsteps striding their way over to him. Gil dared not move, but he had to do something. His eyes darted around for anything he could use. He soon found the burnt scabbard of his sword, it was several feet away. Gil decided that without his parents to help him, this was his best chance. As quick as he could, he lunged toward the sword, drew it, and pointed it at the new threat. Heart pounding, vision blurry, Gil could see a large, gruff middle aged man with a lumbering stature, long dark hair, and a great scar across his face. The man paused. After a moment, Gil realized the man was wearing a large, black cloak, and had a dark horse. Fear crept into Gil's heart, his pulse now racing. The dark rider stood completely still. He soon lifted something to his face. It was the Lamb. The rider smiled a crooked smile.

"Tell me, *boy*," the rider sneered, "where are the ones who killed my sons?"

Gil said nothing. With teeth clinched, brows furrowed, he widened his stance, ready to spring forth.

"I already know I have the one who killed my youngest son, this gifted lamb here. I can smell it, it is *the* Lamb," the rider said. Gil's heart sank as fear further engulfed him. Then, he found his nerve.

"If you must blame anyone for the deaths of your sons, let it be me. I'll strike you down just as I did your youngest!" said Gil. The scarred man started to laugh.

"I know it wasn't *you* who killed them, but you *will* be the first to die as compensation!" he snarled, then threw the Lamb to the side.

It landed with a thud and lay motionless. Gil became enraged; the dark rider drew his sword. His blade was dripping with an evil aura, a spiritual essence of sorts. Gil's sword responded by becoming engulfed with golden flame.

"Another supernatural blade? So I guess this really *is* the Lamb. It will make a fitting sacrifice to lord Varcilyc," he said.

At this, Gil lunged toward the man in black with all his might. Gil struck at him, but was blocked by the corrupt blade. The rider used the hilt of his sword to counter Gil's and delivered a deep slice into his abdomen. Gil leapt back and cringed with pain. As he held his injury, he found not just intense bleeding, but an almost ravenous acidic infection!

"Just give up now, boy!" the scarred man said, "you'll suffer less!"

Gil struggled to stand as he lifted his blade once more. For a fleeting moment, he glanced to one side. The Lamb was now standing and alertly watching him in his struggle. With a loud scream, Gil rushed the rider. With a mighty swing, he broke the dark blade. Gil's sword followed through to hit its mark. The rider fell to the ground in two smoldering pieces. Gil then collapsed and blacked out.

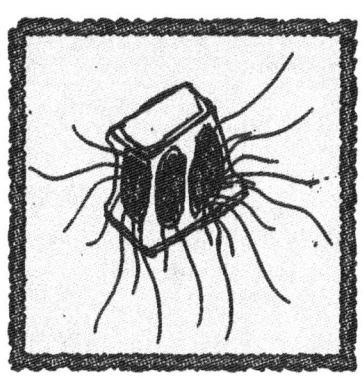

The Black Box

Gil awoke groggily. He found himself laying on the ground with his head resting on his mother's lap. Mera smiled tenderly down at him.

"It's alright, sweetie," she said, "momma's got you ... It's alright."

Looking around, he could see his father, Salderith, Spindley, and the Lamb. He jerked as the memories of what had just transpired rushed back to him. He looked at the corpse of the dark rider, then at his own injury. It was gone! The wound had disappeared!

"But," Gil started, "he got me. I fought the rider and he sliced my belly open."

"Well, you're healed now," said Bregal.

"Yes," said Spindley, "judging by the tear in your clothes, it was a pretty nasty slash."

"What about the infection?" asked Gil.

"What infection?" asked Mera.

"That rider, he-he had a sword of darkness! It was covered in it, and when it hit me, it felt like it was eating my flesh!"

"Oh my!" said Spindley. "You're lucky to be alive, dear. That sounds like a dragon spit blade. A skilled wielder could take out an entire village! Its poison infects all who touch it."

"How could I have made it, the-..." Gil trailed off as he searched for the Lamb again. It was still there beside him.

"When Spindley dug us out," started Bregal, "we found it standing over you."

Gil reached out to it, the Lamb stepped forward to meet his hand. He cradled its head and gently pet it.

"We should get indoors," said Spindley.

"But it's gone," said Gil, "it's all gone, the rider blew it up."

"Oh, dear," said Spindley, "he only got the cottage. The rest of our home is quite fine. Besides, Sal needed another project to work on anyway."

Bregal helped Gil onto his feet, and they all headed to where the small cottage once stood. The spiral staircase was still intact, and they all made their way back down to the dining hall once more.

After taking their seats at the beautiful, almost alive, table, Spindley treated them with a hearty stew of sorts. It was rather mushy with lots of different plants, but had plenty of hot, savory spices in it. Shortly into the meal, Spindley brought out some tall mugs.

"This is my prized spiced fangroot tea!" said Spindley.

Bregal let out a yelp as he drank the tea, Mera almost choked on hers. Gil just took the tiniest sip, a flurry of fiery sweetness, then soothing coolness filled his senses, and cleared his nostrils.

"Glad you like it!" said Spindley. "It's been some time since I last had an excuse to brew this much.

The clans would burrow miles from the far east just for a taste."

Sal half smiled at Gil, while grabbing for his cup. And while Spindley was going on, he slowly poured his tea on the ground.

"Yes," Spindley went on, "we Hofkin really do love the taste of fangroot. The Stickly's and the Pricklebottoms used to fight whenever it ran short."

"Are they still around?" asked Gil.

"No …" said Spindley, now filled with melancholy. "They're all gone, although, I hope not dead. See, when the dragon got word we were housing a fugitive, Ol' Sal over there, he torched our land with his terrible fire. I believe some escaped to the east, our homeland, but many died. His fire was so great, it baked us in our tunnels. Me and Sal barely made it. Just luck, really." She looked down, then whipped around and bustled back to the kitchen. All at the table was silent. Once Spindley came back, Mera spoke up.

"Did you grow these herbs and spices yourself?"

"Why, yes I did!" said Spindley, now pleasant. "I grow all the plants and such we'll ever need right here in the tunnels!"

Sal gurgled and grumbled a bit.

"That's the first good idea you've had all day, dear!" said Spindley. "I'll show you!"

They all got up from the table and followed Spindley down a winding tunnel, then veered into a corridor to the side. They entered a large room with a vast array of plant life. It was all illuminated by a large crystal in the center. Looking up, there were large growths of glowing mushrooms on the ceiling.

"Welcome to my garden," said Spindley.

"Wow!" said Mera. "How can all this thrive so well?"

"Well," said Spindley, "see that crystal there? My people believed that everything in this world has its own song, so to speak. We can't hear most of the songs of the world, but sometimes we can see or feel them. Rare stones tend to give off the strongest tones of the songs. That crystal provides light for the whole garden. But it still isn't quite like the sun, so, after a lot of failures, I found a mushroom that gives the rest of what these plants need to survive down here."

Bregal let out a subtle sigh. Mera heard it though, she gave him a little prod with her elbow.

"That's really something …" said Bregal.

"Thank you!" said Spindley. "Now, let's have some desert!" she turned and started leading them back to the dining hall. On the way, Mera leaned over and whispered to Bregal.

"I wish you'd be a bit more opened minded sometimes... Even if you don't believe it, the least you could do is listen." Bregal replied with another sigh.

Once back in the large hall, they found the Lamb standing on the table. It seemed like it was waiting for their return. It was standing on Sal's spot.

"Better go get it," whispered Mera to Gil.

Gil headed that way, but Sal was ahead of him. Sal reached to gather his empty bowl and silverware, when the Lamb breathed gold right into his mouth. Startled, he stepped back and stumbled to the ground. Mera gasped, and Spindley exclaimed, "Sal!" A brief moment later, he stood back up.

"I'm fine, pricklebear," spoke Sal. "I'm fine thanks to this little one." He turned to the Lamb. Sal pet its head and said, "thank you, thank you so much." Tears started to stream down his face. Spindley rushed to Sal, sobbing in a hurried hobble. She held him in a big hug.

"Oh, Sal! I've waited so long to hear you call me that!" Spindley then turned to the Lamb. "Thank you so much, dear."

The Bringer family stood back as the two coped with their newfound miracle. Bregal stood silent, Mera was in tears, and Gil let a couple drips roll down his face.

Later, the Bringers where begged to stay the night, so they did. Spindley took them down a series of tunnels that led to what looked like an old bunkhouse for guests and company. There they enjoyed the depths of silence and solitude that the dark of a tunnel or cave brings to one who longs for deep sleep. In the morning, Spindley came and woke them. Once back in the dining hall, Spindley and Sal served them breakfast. It was another unusual dish, a roasted wild bird of sorts, and spicy gravy with odd crunchy bits in it. All was silent at the start of the meal, when Sal spoke.

"Would you like to hear a story, the story of how the dragons came into this world?" he asked.

"Sure," said Bregal.

"There is a legend," Sal started, "that a dark spirit was cast down to terra. It was imprisoned in the depths of the ground and stone. There it stayed while terra itself started to take its true form and life blossomed in all areas of its surface. The land where the spirit was banished became home to a race of lizard-like folk called the Veptkeep. The Veptkeep were a peaceful people, great farmers and tradesmen. Their flame breath was really only good for lighting candles or campfires. They were living in a time of splendor in a garden that was a paradise. Then one day, while exploring a ravine, the Veptkeep found the trapped spirit. The Black Box, they called it. It told them many secrets, how to get power, how to get wealth, how to get more. Eventually they moved its housing to their hub village where all could worship and receive their answers to whatever questions they may have." Sal paused for a moment. "As time went on though," he continued, "they became a race of anger and strength, then an empire always lusting for more. My family was in one of the colonies to the Northeast. My grandfather told me our family never worshipped the spirit, and that's why we were stuck in the colony, in exile to resist our corrupt culture. He also used to say that back in the motherland, the Black Box was distorting our people. They grew large, strong, ruthless and beast-like, their flames grew to be like mighty torches that could turn bone to ash!

"At some point though," he went on, "a very nasty scheme was put into action. There was a great tournament, a battle to the death to decide who would rule the kingdom. After much bloodshed, one was victorious, he was the largest and mightiest in the land. The poor creature had clawed his way to the top, then at the ceremony, the high priests bound and sacrificed him on top of the Black Box. It cracked. The dark spirit was freed from the box and took on a new host. He claimed himself Varcilyc, ruler of the drakes. He went on to wage war on all the nations, and even hunt down his own kind. My family and a few others had kept away from the Black Box and all it offered, but that made us a target for the new ruler's wrath. All who were not distorted by the box were hunted down, mutilated, and killed. They killed my family in front of me, and took my tongue. I should be dead right now, but somehow, I got away. I wandered around the wilderness until I found the most beautiful creature," he turned to Spindley.

"Even though he couldn't speak to say it," she said, "I could tell what he felt. And I'd never seen such a handsome, yet injured creature in all my life!"

They held hands while sitting together and stared into each other. They closed their eyes and rubbed their noses together. Sal turned back to the table.

"Her parents took care of me, and after a while, we were wed. Years later, they found out where I was, and burned down the village, and killed most of our people. Like she was saying, I hope some made it out, but we're not sure," he stared down for a moment.

"Have you thought about looking for them?" asked Gil.

"We have, dear," said Spindley, "we just can't go very far out, we're just not as young as we used to be. We can't haul very much on foot for very long."

Bregal held Mera as they sat, still processing the story.

"What about the rider's horse?" said Bregal. "He won't be needing it anymore. And if that's the head of the pack, I doubt anyone will come looking for him."

"Bregal!" shouted Mera. "That's morbid!"

"What?" he said. "That's what we did."

"Those were different circumstances!" she said.

"He may be right, Mera," said Sal. "We would fare much better on horseback. Maybe we *could* look for survivors."

Shortly afterwards, the Bringers were loaded to set out on the road once again. They told Spindley and Sal of their meeting time and place with the men of Bejavia, but the elderly couple seemed preoccupied with a newfound perspective of hope.

"Thank you all so much!" said Spindley. Tears trickling down her fuzzy little cheeks.

"We hope to see again someday! Take care!" said Sal.

As the wagon rolled over the ashen hills, the couple waved goodbye to the ones who had changed their lives. They went on to rebuild their little home-front, and explore the vast forests of the east.

"I hope they'll be alright," said Gil.

"I'm sure they will, dear," said Mera. "After all, they've been blessed by the Provider."

As they traveled, they soon found themselves in the lush variety of colors of the forest in fall. The clouds began to lift and the sun beamed through the tree tops. Birds began to sing and small forest animals began to scurry about in the newfound warmth. For a few hours, none spoke. Although well rested, there was still much to consider.

"Look at all this beauty!" Mera thought to herself. "Look at all this life! This world is still so full and beautiful. We must push forward! Not just for me, but for him" she turned to Gil and slowly put a hand on his shoulder. He jumped a little, as if he'd been pulled out of a trance. With warmth on her face and gentleness in her tone, she said, "I love you, son."

"I love you too, Mom" said Gil. He then turned back to the spot in the woods he had been staring at before. "Is it that obvious?" he wondered to himself. "There's so much darkness in this world … can we really win? Do we even stand a chance? Are we gonna make it? It seems like where ever we go, death is waiting." He looked down where his belly had been slashed, then at the Lamb that lay on his lap. "I should be dead," he thought to himself. "I should be, but I'm not. That must count for something, right? But I've never killed anyone before. I don't think I've ever been more scared in my life! I don't think I'll ever be able to forget it! I can still see it, see it all. I can-. "

"I'm proud of you, son," Bregal called over his shoulder. "I'm sorry you had to go through all that," he went on, "I'd hoped to keep this feeling from you as long as I could. You see, son, even in self-defense, or defending others, taking a life isn't easy. Your mother and I had to take lives to save our own for years. It may seem like I have a heart of stone sometimes, but we remember each and every life we've ever taken" he paused for a moment. "It's not like killing an animal. People have a spirit, and it hurts our spirit to harm another's. Did we make the right choices in taking those lives? I believe so. We'd be dead if we hadn't. But every time we do, we give up a little piece of ourselves in the process. It's like your granddad Elkvich said. It's the wounds that you can't see that hurt the most."

"Is that what this is?" asked Gil. "I'm wondering if I should still be alive. It's like my soul is on fire."

"Oh, Gilly!" said Mera.

Tears streamed down her face as she embraced him. Gil started to sob. As he did, a small tongue started to lick his cheeks. Gil felt the turmoil die down as a sense of a soft soothingness started to calm his heart. He opened his eyes to see the Lamb staring back into him. It had droplets of water rolling down its face. "Were those my tears?" thought Gil.

"In time," Bregal went on, "the Provider has a way of making things work out. These new feelings may go away, or they might not. Either way, try to trust that the Provider is still using you to shape this world," Bregal paused for a moment. "Son, you must understand, even though you feel like you're small, your impact is bigger than you could ever know. We all will be held responsible for all we do and don't do. I vowed to protect my family or die trying. Whatever may come down the road, I will fight. It is my duty and my honor to protect the ones I love," Bregal had a straight face, but Gil could see a tear streak down his cheek.

"And I vowed to help him and watch his back through anything!" Mera said. "A good man needs a good woman by his side!" She lovingly placed a hand on Bregal's back. While holding the reigns in one hand, Bregal reached back and held Mera's hand.

After a few moments, Gil asked. "Dad, where are we going?"

"Ember city, son," he said, "the capital. Hopefully the men of Bejavia will already be there."

As they finally emerged from the Iron Oak Forest, dusk's soft hue began to engulf the prairies and groves along the roadside. The trees were thick in patches, and several farms and fields could be seen in the distance. Bregal suddenly sat up in his seat.

"Weapons ready," he whispered.

"Hm?" said Mera.

She peaked over his shoulder and saw a tattered young man with a bright, smiling face. He was waving to them in a friendly manner.

"Hello there!" he called. "Might I trouble you for a ride, it wouldn't be far!" Bregal slowed the wagon a good distance away.

"I don't like this," muttered Bregal.

"Oh, Breg," said Mera, "he doesn't seem dangerous. Besides, there's three of us, and one of him."

"But mom," said Gil, "maybe he's baiting us …"

"Yes!" said Bregal, "And he may not *seem* dangerous, but his buddies might!"

"Breg … it isn't anything we can't handle … Let's give him a ride," she said.

"But it's getting dark!" protested Bregal.

"So we'll just have to have him stay for dinner!" she said.

"What!" said Bregal.

"Mom … Why?" groaned Gil.

"Oh, hello!" called Mera. "We'll take you as far as Ember City, but it's getting dark! After a while we'd like to make camp and have some dinner! Would you care to join us?" The young man put on an even cheerier face.

"Oh, I'd love to!" he said.

The young man limped over and hopped into the wagon. Bregal muttered something under his breath. Mera flicked the back of his head in response. The young man was a bit older than Gil, had dirty stubble, long blonde hair, and ragged clothes.

"Thanks for having me," he said. Mera smiled warmly.

"Not a problem! So, what's your name?" she asked.

"It's Jenneth, Jenneth Wricklevern," his smile still shone brightly.

"Well, Jenneth, I'm Mera, this is my husband, Bregal, and our son, Gil," neither Gil or Bregal responded, Jenneth seemed unfazed though.

"Huh, and who's this little one?" he asked, reaching toward the Lamb. Gil grabbed it and held it tightly to his chest. "Oh, sorry, I was just going to pat its head."

"It's fine," said Mera, "it's just, this little one is our only livestock left."

"I'm sorry, did the dragon take them?" he asked.

"No, we just had to sell everything so we'd be prepared for our journey," she said.

"Journey?" he asked.

"Yes, we're headed to Ember City from the far plains, beyond the Iron Oak Forest," she said. Gil still held the Lamb close, but kept a finger or two on his sword. Their guest seemed to be unarmed, but he didn't want to chance it.

"I'm afraid Ember City's lost," he said.

"Really?" Mera asked.

"Well, in a way. The people there are obsessed with consuming and collecting," he said, a bit down hearted.

"Greed?" asked Mera.

"Yes, among other things …" his upbeat eagerness became a bit watered down and his gaze drifted to the side. He was suddenly rather distant.

There wasn't much talking after that, Jenneth's demeanor didn't really change. Eventually they made camp and Mera cooked a hearty meal over the fire. The stars shone brightly overhead, everything seemed at ease and still. Jenneth remained in his melancholy state. Mera approached him with a bowl of stew; she flashed her lovely smile as he met her gaze.

"It's my own recipe, eat up!" she said warmly. He slowly took the bowl.

"Thanks …" he said.

After handing him the bowl, she sat down next to Bregal. Mera felt puzzled at their guest's lack of enthusiasm. Then Jenneth stood up and looked out into the surrounding brush and trees.

"Hey … not these ones," he said. A dozen or so men slowly emerged here and there from the thicket into the light of the fire. A large haggard man with a scar across his face approached Jenneth.

"You sure, Jenneth?" he asked.

"Yeah, they're just as well off as we are. Plus, they're good folk, good folk are hard to come by anymore …" he said. The large man stroked his long dark beard for a moment. Bregal and Gil slowly reached for their weapons.

"Alright, not them," he finally said.

Bregal and Gil relaxed their grip. The small mob began to retreat back into the brush when Mera sprang up.

"Boys!" she called out. The men all stopped. Bregal shot Mera a look. "Don't you want some dinner?" she asked. The big, bearded man turned to her.

"Thanks ma'am, but we have families to get back to," his tone was soft and almost defeated sounding.

"Well, just take the pot!" she said. All the men, including Bregal looked at her with surprise. "Yes, take it with you!" she said. Jenneth turned to face Mera.

"Mera, you'd really do that … after we were going to rob you?" he asked. She smiled warmly.

"You were, but you didn't, so yes, I am! Go feed you families," she said. The group of men were dumbfounded.

"You-you sure?" asked the large man. Mera just kept her sweet smile as answer.

One of the other men slowly came forward and retrieved the large pot full of stew. He stepped back in with the other men.

"Well, Boys!" shouted the dark bearded man. "What do we say!"

"Thank you!" they all shouted simultaneously, then retreated back into the thicket. Jenneth slowly looked back over his shoulder before disappearing out of sight.

Mera slowly turned to see Bregal's disgruntled frown. Her smile disappeared and she stuck her nose up and looked away from him.

"Don't start, dear," she said.

"Ok … but nice job," he said. She glance back to see his frown melt into a smile. She smiled back as she dug through their bags trying to find more food.

"I love you," Bregal said. Mera paused and stared up into his eyes, her gaze was soft.

"I love you too," she said tenderly.

A bit later, Gil drifted asleep while his parents lay on the other side of the fire. The Lamb snoozed happily along side him. They all slept well that night, although a bit hungry.

Ember City

After a long week on the road, they finally reached the gates of Ember City. It was huge; its expanse wide and its buildings tall. The proud wall and gate jutted from the ground like cliffs! As they neared the entrance, they could see the flame-like amber colors of the buildings and the jagged, fire themed architecture. The lampposts were great blazing torches. Even the people dressed in fire-like garb with many different shades of yellows, reds, and oranges. The gate opened up to the square where hundreds of folk bustled about. There was much energy, but no laughter or joy, just frantic, aggressive grumbling and yelling. They fought and yelled over small trinkets, even when they'd have to struggle to make room to fit any more on their bodies.

A strange scent seemed to linger in the dense, warm air. On inhale, Gil could taste smoke … and iron. Mera held herself and rubbed her arms as an eerie feeling started to creep in. Something about the chalky textured buildings and road made her… uneasy. Bregal experienced similar sensations, but ignored it for the most-part.

Bregal peered into the crowd, watching for an opening. The moment one appeared, he jolted old Walnut into a trot with a swift smack on her rear. The horse and wagon flew through the crowd. Bregal, doing his best to steer, ended up flinging the wagon this way and that until he had had enough. Bregal suddenly pulled the reigns tight, and Walnut scrambled to an abrupt stop. This sent Mera, Gil, and the Lamb tumbling into the wall of the wagon.

"You guys alright?" asked Bregal.

"Yeah, I'm fi-" Gil started.

"What on terra do you think you're doin, Breg!" Mera shouted. "You nearly killed us!"

"Woman!" he started. "I saw and opening and I took it!"

"Don't you, *woman*, me! Someone could have gotten hurt!" she said. "And so much for trying to keep a low profile!"

"You can't just let me steer, can ya!" he said.

"Not when you put us in danger, Bregal! You're lucky I-" she stopped as a short stranger in a cloak approached them.

"Bregal?" the voice was of a stout old man. "It's me, it's Rolldrin."

Bregal's face brightened. "Rolld-!"

"Sh … not so loud!" Rolldrin said. He then glanced around. "Grab your things, leave the rest behind. Hurry!"

The Bringers grabbed everything but left Ol' Walnut

and the wagon behind. He led them down a series
of alleys and into an old cellar. Once there, they were
met by the men of Bejavia and a dozen others. An old
woman approached them.

"Rolldrin, were you followed?" she asked.

"No, I'm sure of it," he said.

"These are them? The Bringers? Elkvich's line?" she asked.

"Yes, ma'am," Rolldrin said. The old woman stepped
closer, eyeing them.

"Yes, I can see it. You look a lot like him, Bregal,"
she said.

"You know me?" asked Bregal.

"I was there when you were born, so yes, I do," she said.

"Velera?" asked Bregal. The old woman slowly
smiled a warm smile.

"I'm surprised you remember, Bregal. It's been so long."

"With how dad would go on and on about you, I
sometimes wondered if you were my *real* mother," he said.

"Oh!" she laughed. "I'm afraid Elkvich wasn't really
my type. Besides, your mother was the sweetest woman
I'd ever met. It was a gift just to be near her."

"You're talking about grandma?" asked Gil.

"Yes, dear," Mera gently hugged him from the side.

"I never knew her," Gil said. Velera turned to Gil,
still smiling.

"She was kind and loving, gentle and strong. I
looked up to her most of my life. But in the end, she
was truly fierce. People said she had the strength of
ten men that day. She held the way so that I and many
others could survive. I'll never forget her." She paused
for a moment. "Well, you're all here now. We discovered
your friends the other day, they were headed for trouble
in the marketplace when we found them, and they told
us all about you." Bregal turned to Rolldrin.

"Rolldrin, you were a Keeper the whole time?"

"Sorry about the discretion, Bregal," Rolldrin said. "I knew if the Provider was on your side, you'd find your way here no matter what."

"Now, now," said Velera, "let's all have a seat and get settled in. We have much to discuss."

After a few more moments of bickering, greetings, and reunions, they all sat in a large circle on the floor. Looking around, Gil could see little of the dimly lit cellar. The walls were rough cobble, and the shelves appeared bare and empty. In fact, the only thing worth noting was the deep red rug they were seated on. Gil sat next to his parents on one side, Rolldrin sat on the other side of Bregal and Mera. Gil held onto the Lamb, as it quietly slept in his arms. A moment later, someone sat down next to him. His heart began to race as he realized it was a girl! But not just any girl, a beautiful girl, just about his age. He could hear his mother giggle a bit. Gil could imagine what she might be thinking. He snapped out of it for a moment when Velera started to speak.

"Welcome everyone, to the Keepers. First off, I'd like to announce that our salvation has come! The Lamb has been found!" as she spoke, the group began to cheer. The Lamb jerked its head, then got up and walked toward Velera.

"What a beautiful creation, we're honored to be in your pres-" she was cut short as the Lamb breathed its gold in her mouth. She sat stunned for a moment, then fell backward laughing, then sobbing. Concerned whispers and questions rose from the group. After a few minutes, she sat up. "Thank you," she said, tears streaming down her face. "But who?" The Lamb turned and started back to Gil. On its way there, it looked at the girl next to him, then laid back down again on Gil's lap.

"Great news!" Velera said. "Victory is at hand, all we need to do is walk it out; I was just given a vision of what that looks like. Now, there are some things that are bound to happen, but if we stay strong and true, the Provider has laid our path."

"So, we'll all be alright?" asked one of the men from Bejavia.

"I will not lie to you," she said, "some of my tears were of sadness. If we falter or turn from the path at all, we will be done for. And one of us has been destined to betray the Lamb." A commotion started to rise. "Now, everyone!" she stood up. "Please listen, this is something that has to happen. Keepers, you should already know of what I speak. Besides, we must show love regardless; I will not let this fact split us apart."

"But who is it?" came another voice.

"That's not important," she said, "we just need to be prepared for it when it happens. Be aware, not paranoid."

"I saw it look at Lila!" said someone.

The group erupted with accusations and quarrels. Gil turned to the girl next to him, she was sobbing. He reached out and gently touched her shoulder. She then flung her arms around him and wept. The Lamb lifted its head and licked the tears from her cheeks.

"Enough!" shouted Velera. She took a small mace from her robe and struck it on the ground. A flash of lightning lit up the room. All was silent.

"I will not stand to have this back stabbing in the Provider's house! I know your hearts are broken and cold, but don't you dare lash out! The Provider called us to love one another. I thought that by now, you all had realized this," she said.

"But the Lamb, it looked at her!" said someone.

"I don't care! We must love regardless, not turn on

one another! Even if she *is* the one, we must love her just the same. Look at her, poor thing." Velera stepped across the circle and hugged both Lila and Gil. Gil sat stunned and unsure of what to do. Eventually Lila clung to Velera. A few minutes later, Lila stopped crying and Velera released her, and Velera returned to her place. Lila turned to Gil, tears still slowly trickling down her chin.

"Thank you for your kindness. I know we haven't met yet, but thank you." Gil sat still stunned. Even though she was in tears, her delicate features were still beautiful. Her short, dark hair, her deep blue eyes, and pale skin, these were things Gil hadn't noticed much before. She seemed so beautiful and fragile.

"It's fine …" Gil said sheepishly, "I don't mind," there was an uneasy pause.

"I'm Lila," she said.

"I'm Gilgath," said Gil. Lila giggled a little.

"That's an odd name," she said. His cheeks grew flushed.

"I guess … it's from my mom's language. She's from the Mid Terra Islands."

"Oh, what's it mean?" she asked.

"It means something along the lines of long awaited gift," he said.

"Wow, I'm not sure what my name means …" she looked down for a moment. "The dragon took my parents when I was young."

"Oh … I'm sorry," said Gil.

"It's alright, I was very young. The Keepers became my family," she said, she then looked into Gil's eyes. "I've never really been around anyone my age for very long. They're all either a lot older or a lot younger than me …" she paused for a moment and broke eye contact. "Could I call you Gil?" Gil felt relieved at such a simple question.

"Sure, most people do," he said. She still looked away.

"Can I call you Gilly?" she asked, her face now red. Gil felt a knot in his throat.

"I-I guess, if you want. My mom calls me that sometimes, but you can too if you want."

"Gilly," she said, even quieter now. "Will you be my friend?"

His nerves let up a bit at this question. He felt a little confused though. He had some friends his age here and there before, but never a girl.

"I can, if you want," Gil turned away. Lila secretly smiled a bit and scooted a tiny bit closer to him.

"Children!" Velera raised her voice, Lila and Gil jumped. "I know you have much to talk about, but please pay attention. Especially you, Gil!" The two looked down. Mera smirked and nudged Gil a little. "Now then," Velera went on, "again, for those of you unfamiliar to us, the Living Book tells of a once beautiful spirit. One of many beautiful spirits, and in its arrogance, it rose up against the Provider. The Provider, being limitless and flawless, banished the rebellious spirit from paradise. We believe the drake is a powerful manifestation of that spirit." Gil reacted as if he wanted to talk, but held his tongue. "You have something to share, Gil?" asked Velera.

"Yes, ma'am, the drake *is* that spirit," Gil said. A bit of hushed whispers resounded amongst the congregation.

"How can you be sure?" Velera asked.

"We met someone on our journey," started Bregal, "he's a descendant of the Veptkeep. His family refused the dark spirit and wasn't contorted. He told us a story about his nation and its history."

"Well," Velera said, "let's hear it!"

The Bringers then told the story of the Black Box to all the Keepers.

"That must be why there's only one dragon left!" said Rolldrin. "It must have devoured its own to become powerful enough to take Typhril!"

"Alright, everyone!" said Velera. "We need to discuss our plan of action. We need to act quick but have enough time to properly prepare. I have been given a specific number of days. Six, in six days, we will infiltrate the sewers." Unrest came over the group. "I know what you're thinking, and if we keep to the path, it'll be alright. Your strength *will* be tested though. Once we emerge next to the fortress, we'll rest and attack at dawn. I do believe we should split up. Rolldrin will lead one group and I will lead the other. We both know these channels very well, so we should be fine as long as we keep strong and stay together. On that note, we should all call it a night and get some rest."

The meeting came to a close and everyone found a place to sleep. The Bringers slept next to each other, with Gil on the edge. The Lamb slept snuggled up against him. At one point, Gil opened his eyes to see Lila sleeping a short distance away. He could reach out to her if he wanted to. He did want to, but didn't. He stared at her, then drifted back to sleep.

Once morning came, all the Keepers sat together and had a rather crude and basic breakfast, then proceeded into several songs of praise to the Provider with various instruments. Then the different members would talk and mingle until the next meal time, then again till supper, then Velera would talk of the old days and read from the Living Book, then bed. And over the course of these next days, friendships were struck, wounds began to heal, and some things received clarity.

On one of these days, around a meal, Gil sat with Velera and asked, "Velera, what is the Living Book?" she smiled warmly.

"It's a book that's been studied and passed down for generations, it's the word of the Provider. You see, Gil, when the dragon took the throne, he did away with the old ways and tried to abolish our people's history to make way for … other things. The Living Book is also a collection and testimony of man's relationship with the Provider. The picture on the cover comes from the seeing prophet, Heggile, he wrote a hymn to go along with it too. Let's see if I can remember…" she thought for a moment then began softly singing.

"Dark the flame starts, then to crimson
Crimson in turn fades red
Red then changes into orange
Orange, yellow, then to gold!

Coals and embers, then start roaring
Scorch the fears of the unknown
Breath the breath of Silver Lion
Till we find our everlasting home!

And so spins,
And so spins
the fire of our souls

Broken hearts of generations
Fought and died for our King
Hope endures till salvation
What a sight to behold!

Doubts and failures mean but nothing
Blood and spirit make us whole
Stand up in the face of tyrants
Till the day we're given our promise stone

And so spins,
And so spins
The fire of our souls!"

"Pretty, is this the last one, the last Living Book?" he asked. She looked down for a moment."

"There used to be more, but yes, to my knowledge, this is the last one," she said. Gil strayed away in thought for a moment.

"Gil!" Velera said at last. He jumped a little. "Have you ever heard of having a relationship with the Provider?"

"Not really, my parents don't talk about that stuff too much," he said.

"Well," she went on, "one of our core beliefs is that our closeness to the Provider is up to us. See this little mace of mine?" She held out her small metallic mace. Its blunt nobs glistened in the dim light of the lanterns and candles that littered the cellar.

"Yeah," he said.

"When I was young, I sought the Provider with all I had. I attended the daily readings and praisings, memorized segments of the Living Book, whatever I could. And even though it was frowned upon for a girl to be as such, I didn't care! However, it still wasn't enough. I started focusing too much on doing things. Then, one day, in desperation, I went up to the snowy peaks of the north. I desperately pleaded to the Provider, pouring my heart out to Him. "What must I do to be with you!" I shouted, then a mighty storm came, and in the storm, I heard a whisper. "Are you done trying, or do you want to start being?" It asked. "Being!" I said. Then I felt an urge. I found a stone buried in the snow, I picked it up and held it high. A great bolt of lightning struck the rock and it was transformed! It became this mace. I heard the voice again. "Take the tools you have been given and do my works, the day is coming when you will see my perfect gift to all creation," she paused for a moment. "And so, I did."

On another day, Gil sat next to Lila again.

"So, this is what your life's like, huh?" Gil asked.

"Well, not always … Sometimes it's better, usually it's worse though," she said.

"Yeah?"

"Yeah, I try to have a better view of things, but it's hard sometimes."

"I bet."

"What-what was life like for you?" Gil looked away to the floor. Lila jerked a little.

"It's OK, Gil!" she said. "You don't have to talk about it if you don't want to!"

"It's fine, it's just it feels like it's been so long … But I used to live in our clan's homestead. We had a bunch of different animals and we lived in peace on the countryside." Gil looked up to see the Lamb prancing around with one of the little kids.

"You had a clan?" Lila asked.

"Well, yeah, but our clan's been separated for a while now. Most of us moved out of the country."

"Oh, sorry."

"It's alright … Have there always been this few Keepers?"

"No, there were a lot of us, but now there's only a couple dozen, not including the children."

"I only see a couple of kids."

"Yeah, they're orphans, like me."

"Sorry."

"I've had to learn to accept it."

"Well, at least we have something to hope in."

"Yeah, at least there's that," she said. A tear started to trickle down to her cheek. Gil hesitantly put a hand on her upper back. She then leaned over and rested her head on his shoulder. "It's nice to have someone my age to talk to," she said.

"Yeah …," Gil said.

On the final night, Gil laid awake with one hand partially extended toward Lila until he drifted to sleep. His dreams were sweet that night. He dreamt of his life. He was married, had two boys and one girl; the sun was bright and warm, and they were happy, full of joy and love. When Gil awoke, he found that his outstretched hand was being gripped. Still asleep, Lila had reached out and held his hand in the middle of the night. Gil felt happy, but withdrew before anyone else could see. Lila soon slowly woke up; she smiled at Gil.

"Good morning," she said. "How did you sleep?" she was smiling rather cheerfully.

"Pretty good, you?" asked Gil.

"Good, I had the most wonderful dream. I was married to a great man, had great children, three in fact, and had a great life with them."

"Wow," he said, "that sounds pretty great." He giggled a little, so did she.

"Come on you two," Velera said, standing over them. "We need to get going." She smiled at them for a moment.

The group gathered, then divided in two. Rolldrin would lead the Bringers, and the men of

Bejavia, while Velera would lead the rest, about two dozen per party. The few small children in their group hung from a couple stouter archers in packs.

"Everyone be careful, be on guard at all times!" said Velera. "Look to the Provider for strength and you will be strong. I will see you soon; may the Provider bless and keep us."

With that, they parted. Both squads found a separate entryway to the sewers, just off the streets. Rolldrin lit a torch once they were all down.

"Follow me," he said, "and stay close, no matter what, stay close to the light … We're not alone down here." An uneasiness set in as the group started forward.

"Rolldrin, what do you mean by not alone?" asked Bregal.

"There are evil creatures that roam these tunnels. Few live after coming in contact with one. They're ghoulish things of darkness; they hate the light, so they lure people into the dark to devour them. They're called cave sirens; some of the most wicked spawn to walk terra."

"How awful!" said Mera.

"Aye, and they're not just here; they reside under most cities anymore," he went on. "Bregal, you remember that axe? The one that belonged to that young man I told you about?"

"Yes …" Bregal said.

"Turns out, he got drunk one night in Hallowburg and stumbled down into its depths. That's why the axe ended up there. When I approached his family, the boy's father somehow already heard and went looking for him, and hasn't been seen since. I asked around at Hallowburg on my way here … no one's seen either one return," he paused briefly. "I'd love to kill one of these things, but we need to keep safe."

As they traveled deeper and deeper into the depths of the channels and canals, the scents became almost suffocating, and the darkness itself seemed to stifle any light. The torch stayed the same, but the dark seemed to slowly be overtaking it. It felt like hours had passed, then suddenly one of the men from Bejavia started acting strange. The Lamb started to wriggle in Gil's arms. The man started looking around frantically and began breathing heavily.

"I'm coming, Fira! I'm coming Ness, daddy's coming!" He yelled, then rushed back into the darkness.

"Blair, no!" shouted one of the other men. But it was too late, Blair was out of sight only for a brief moment before his screams of pain and terror filled the tunnels. Several of the men let out sobs at the loss of their friend, and struggled as they pressed forward.

"There's nothing we could have done … I'm sorry, lads," said Rolldrin.

They continued down the sewers. There was a few turns here and there, but Rolldrin assured them they'd be out soon enough. A bit later, Mera started to breath hard.

"Daddy!" she suddenly exclaimed, staring into the dark.

"Honey, no!" said Bregal. "He's dead remember? That's not him, even if it sounds like him, it's not!" she still looked dazed as she peered into the darkness ahead.

"Hey, look at me!" Bregal pleaded. She slowly turned to meet his gaze. "I love you, Mera Bringer, and you're not gonna leave me like this. Snap out of it!"

"Breg?" she said, coming back to reality. "I heard him, he was in pain. He was yelling for my help," she started to weep.

"I know, honey; it's alright, though. You're alright," he said, cradling her in his big arms as she buried herself in his chest.

The Lamb started to wriggle more now. Gil held it tight. Before they started moving again, Gil heard Lila's voice.

"Oh, Gilly …" she said. He looked around confused. The voice came from close behind them. "Gilly? Why don't you come over here?" she went on, her voice was soft and smooth. "Aren't we friends? Aren't we *more*?" Gil tried to ignore the voice. "Gil … come over here in the dark. It's safe and we can be alone together. Wouldn't you like that? I sure would …"

Mera still sobbed in Bregal's arms, the group was still waiting to move on. Gil was struggling not to entertain the voice he heard as reality started to slip away. He could almost see her beautiful face and figure beckoning him in the dark.

"You do *love* me, don't you? Come and make love, we'll be happy together here in the dark." Gil took a step toward the shadows.

The Lamb began to writhe violently in his arms till finally, it fell to the ground. Before it touched the floor, it was no longer Lamb, but Lion. Its great light engulfed the entire tunnel. It roared mightily and a shrieking pale creature fell from the ceiling. The Lion pounced on it, ripping it to shreds. All fear was soon put to rest as the Lion escorted them through and out of the sewers.

The Siege

When they finally emerged, it was night. The others had already made it out. Smiles of reuniting friends and acquaintances were cut short when they learned of their fallen friend.

"Oh, Blair," said Velera, "the poor man." She looked at the rest of the group. "We're blessed to have lost so few to the cave sirens." She looked down for a moment. "I know it's hard to see it now, but it could have been much, much worse. It was last time … When we had to move into that cellar, we took the sewers across the city. We didn't even know those creatures existed … Our numbers were cut in half." All stood silent, save for the weeping of a few men from Bejavia. "Come, let's get some rest."

The group settled in the brush and thicket near the road. Bregal and Mera sat next to a small fire. Still clinging to him, she had stopped weeping but now sat in silence. Amidst the camp, Gil finally found Lila. She sat alone, quietly staring at the ground.

"Hey, you alright?" Gil asked.

She didn't respond. Gil wasn't sure what to do, so he did one of the few things he thought he ought to do. He got down on his knees and hugged her. She burst into tears and hugged him back.

"Gil," she started, "those things, they did such awful things to us! To me! I heard them, they made me hear my parents. They were in pain …They screamed for help in the dark, and they yelled hateful things when I didn't come!"

"Lila," said Gil, "you know that wasn't really them."

"I know, but it *felt* like it was." Tears continued to stream down her face as she held Gil in whimpering silence.

"I bet they'd be proud of you," said Gil.

"What?" she started to release her embrace and looked into his eyes.

"Well, they were Keepers, weren't they?"

"Yeah …"

"Well, I bet they'd be proud of you. After all you've gone through, you're still a strong, beautiful person." He blushed and looked away at realizing what he'd just said.

"Thank you for your kindness," she said. A bit surprised, he turned back to her. She met his gaze even closer now. "Thank you," she said. She leaned forward and closed her eyes. Gil's heart pounded hard in his throat. His head spun with confusion as he realized the shift in their interaction. He still found himself very much drawn to her. As their lips met, they were hit with the rush of their first kiss. It only lasted a moment, but time seemed to stop for them. They soon parted and opened their eyes. They both had red flushed cheeks and turned away from each other bashfully.

"It's getting kind of cold out here, you want to sit next to the fire?" Lila asked.

"Sure, I'm starting to get a little hungry too," Gil said.

The two rejoined the group at the small camp fire. After a few stares from some of the other Keepers, the mood had returned to the state of rest and recuperation. Lila sat next to Velera, and Gil sat next to his parents. Mera reached out for Gil and gave him a big, warm hug.

"We love you very much, son," she said. Then she came in close and whispered, "and I knew you'd find a good one!"

After a late dinner, and some decompressing, the group settled in for a rather frosty night of sleep. There was no orchestra of crickets to serenade them, no moon to shine on the trees, no stars either. All that could be seen was the lights of the city and the smoke from their activities.

The bitter cold greeted them in the morning. The gold light of a fresh sunrise caused the frozen morning dew to glimmer on every dazzling blade of grass. They quickly gathered their things and headed off toward the fortress.

Once there, they saw a great wall and a draw bridge with a cobble arch to meet it. The bridge was up; the group stopped at the edge of the cobble arch. A few moments later, a few men appeared on top of the wall to greet them.

"Who are you, and what is your business with the Great Dragon?" the small soldier asked. His tone was pompous, and he had a rather high pitched voice. Velera stepped out.

"I am Velera, the prophet. I have a message for Varcilyc!" she said.

"How dare you address our king in such a common manner! You shall be-" He was cut short.

"You can tell that overgrown lizard that today is his last! I tell you the truth, the Lamb has come, salvation is here, lay down your arms and join us!" she shouted.

The sentry laughed an odd little chuckle, then turned to the other guards. A moment later, a large ball of fire came hurdling from the fortress down on the them! A few of the Keepers rushed forward and blew large horns of all sorts; the ball of flame haulted mid-air, then was launched back over the wall exploding with a loud boom!

"So be it," said Velera.

She took out her small mace and struck the ground with it. On a clear sunny morning, lightning struck and demolished the wall of the fortress. The rubble made a clear path for them into the courtyard of the castle. As they marched, Rolldrin stepped in front. He pulled out a large drum and began to play. Its tone was deep and the beat was like a great heart. As he played, the troops began to kneel and submit. A mysterious force had touched their hearts. Once across the courtyard, the enemy soldiers began to chant.

"All hail the Lamb … Praise the Provider …" they chanted over and over.

The large double doors of the grand hall opened. A priestess came sprinting out. She looked terrified and out of breath.

"You fools! How could you let trespassers in like-" she stopped and looked around.

Hate grew on her face; she screamed and raced to the Keepers. As she lifted her hands, a wave of ice launched from her. Gil could feel warmth coming from his scabbard. His sword emitted gold fire again. Without thinking, Gil drew his blade and rushed to meet the frozen onslaught. His sword burned intensely as he thrust the blade deep into the ice. A great beam of gold flame turned the frost wave to steam! It burned straight through to the dragon priestess. She shrieked, and fell to the ground as a charred corpse. Gil picked the Lamb back up and they all rushed inside.

The great hall was empty, save a few suits of armor and some decorum. Flags of fire and paintings of darkness hung here and there on the walls. As they walked, they started to get an eerie feeling.

"Something's not right here …" said Velera. She looked up. Following the large marble columns to the distant ceiling, they disappeared into thick darkness. She readied her small mace again.

"Begone, darkness! You are revealed!" she shouted and struck the ground several times. With every strike, a shriek resounded from above their heads. She kept smacking the floor till finally, a giant creature fell from the ceiling and landed with a loud thud. It slowly rose to its feet. It had a large stag skull for a head, the jaws of a great wolf, and the body of a tall man, except it was contorted, a mutilated conglomeration of different corpses. The dark creature stood taller than two men! The Keepers stood in a trance of horror and disgust. It peered at them with hollow eyes, then let out a deafening screech.

"How much blood went into creating such an abomination?" whispered Velera.

The shambling giant reached deep into its ribs and pulled out a long, black blade coated with dark fluid. Essence gushed out onto the ground and its spindly fingers dripped with residue.

"Archers, fire!" called Rolldrin.

A barrage of arrows flew to the creature. It flung its sword and the essence on its blade dissolved the arrows mid flight. Mera struggled to loose her arrow at seeing everyone's failed attempts. She, instead, grabbed Gil and Lila and ran for cover behind one of the pillars. Bregal stayed put.

"Use your mace!" shouted Rolldrin.

The beast peered at them once again, it focused on Velera, who was still out in front of the group.

"Velera, come back, run!" called Bregal, stepping forward.

It bolted at her and flung its great sword. Velera fell to the ground. The creature towered over her; she looked to where Lila was hiding. The old prophet smiled weakly and lifted a hand toward her. Lila could see Velera mouth the words "I love you" as the creature brought down its sword into her spine. She coughed up some blood, then stopped moving. Lila shrieked and tried to run to her, but Gil and Mera held her back. Rolldrin looked on in horror.

"You!" he shouted, lunging over to it. "I'll send you back to the depths, you horrid freak!"

With that, he took a swing at it with one of his shields. The dark giant blocked with its sword, then Bregal swung with the other hand, uppercutting it in the jaw. The monstrosity staggered back, stunned. Bregal sprang forward and landed a nasty blow to the beast's skull. It cracked! The creature shrieked again, then hit Bregal with a backhanded swipe. He went flying into a pillar, then lay motionless. Mera screamed; Rolldrin brought up his great axe and lead a charge with the men of Bejavia. They shouted as they rushed the beast before it could kill Bregal too.

They engaged, several men were swung about as the creature's rage ensued. It flung its sword with such strength that limbs were broken just from blocking it!

Gil looked at his father's motionless body, then at his mother, tears now streaming from her eyes. The Lamb nudged her bow and eagerly looked at her.

"Mom," said Gil, "you have to shoot it!"

"What?" she said through the tears.

"Look at the Lamb," said Gil. She looked down at it. It was eagerly looking her in the eyes. "Mom, it has to be *you*, shoot it and kill it!"

"But none of the other arrows made a difference!" she said.

"But yours might, mom! Aim for the crack dad made in its skull!" said Gil.

"Please, Mrs. Bringer, please end this," sobbed Lila.

Mera's tears stopped. She took her bow, knocked an arrow, drew the string, and took aim at her target. She focused and inhaled deep, then held her breath and waited for the right shot. At one point, Rolldrin cleaved into the creature's ankle. It paused as if wincing with pain. Mera loosed her arrow; it became engulfed with light as it flew to meet its mark. The beast went to block it, but the projectile shattered the corrupt sword! The arrow of light then punctured the creature's skull. The dark giant screamed and fell to its knees, then convulsed violently as it began to dissolve till there was nothing left.

Mera rushed to Bregal's side, Gil soon followed. Lila and Rolldrin came to Velera's corpse. The Lamb breathed on Bregal and revived him. The three cried as they rejoiced.

"Don't let anyone tell you your old man can't take a punch, son!" said Bregal; they chuckled a little, then embraced one another.

The Lamb was brought to all who were wounded. Then, it was brought to Velera. It slowly walked up to her corpse. The Lamb licked her cheek, then tenderly nuzzled its face against hers. A droplet of water trickled to the floor from its face.

"Why isn't it healing her?" asked Lila. All the adults stood silent. "Why? Why isn't she alive right now?" she went on, "How could she die?" She turned to the Lamb. "The only parents I have are dead, and you do *nothing*? *How*?" Rolldrin stepped forward and held her.

"Lila, I know it's hard, but Velera had a rich and full life. If the Lamb hasn't revived her, it must be her time." He said.

"Who says? Who says it's her time? Who decides!" she yelled.

"I believe the Provider decides such things, and the Lamb would never go against the Provider's plan. It was simply her time, Lila … She's in paradise now." Rolldrin looked to the men of Bejavia as Lila sobbed in his arms. "If anyone knows about loss, it's us, we've lost much just like you have. We're here for you, lass."

Lila looked up into Rolldrin's eyes and saw several tears rolling down his perky, round cheekbones.

"I guess you're right," she said. She slowly got up. "Besides, she'd want us to finish this."

The rest of them gave a nod of agreement. Rolldrin moved Velera's corpse to one side and covered it with his cloak. The Keepers set out further into the fortress.

They made their way past several halls and chambers. Many were set up with various dark trinkets, ceremonial garb and instruments and other unsettling things. They eventually found their way to a set of huge golden doors.

"Alright lads," started Rolldrin, "this looks like it. Stay together, and keep strong! Remember, the path has been laid, we just need to keep walking!"

"For the Lamb!" exclaimed one of the men of Bejavia.

"For our loved ones!" said one of the other Keepers.

"And for our world!" said Mera.

Rolldrin took a deep breath as he slowly opened the great doors to the throne room. It was in dismay, it had been turned into a dragon's den! There was a gaping hole in the ceiling, and a huge mound of gold where the throne once stood. Much blood lay splattered all over the floor. The smell of death and decay lingered in the stale air. The drake lay on its plunder. It was gigantic! Its wings could span the room, its claws and fangs as big as a man, and its scales were rotted black with hints of deep crimson. It raised its head as they entered.

"*Well*, what a surprise. I wasn't expecting guests." Its voice was a deep form of garbled growl, and echoed in its own hollowness. The Keepers all took cover behind some pillars. "I'm afraid there's not much point in hiding, I can smell you, and my flame would easily reach you," all but Gil, Lila and the Lamb stepped forward.

"There we are!" Now, before I kill you, I *am* curious of how you made it this far," it said.

"We've come to destroy you, drake!" barked Rolldrin.

"A *dwarf*? Hm, well I guess my old minions missed a few of you after all! No matter … *king of ashes* …" It sneered then paused a moment. Rolldrin yelled as He and several others rushed forward and started bashing and slashing at the dragon. The archers opened fire. "Well, you made it through my wall, my priestess *and* dark guardian ... But *who are you?*" A few arrows bounced off its scales. It took a big sniff. "Ah, I know, the leftovers from Bejavia! That guardian was a product of your little town ... Wait a minute, who freed you?" It looked closely at them. "The Bringers, of course, I smell blessings upon you ... but none from me. And since you came with the Keepers, you must have brought *it*." The drake flung its huge arm and sent them all flying to the wall. The party then laid in a mangled heap on the floor.

"Come on out if you don't want to watch your friends and family burn before your eyes!" the drake said. It blew a burst of black fire into the air.

"Wait!" called Gil. He and Lila slowly stepped out into the open.

"No, Gil!" yelled Bregal.

"Ah, after all these years I can finally be rid of you!" snarled the drake. It reeled back and let out a torrent of dark flame. The great marble pillars caught up in the blast cracked from the stress of the heat and came crashing down to the floor. When the flame finally ceased, the three remained untouched!

"What!" yelled the dragon. It tried again and again, till even the stone floor cracked, but to no avail. It perked its head a bit, then relaxed. "Little girl, are your parents Thounen and Kinira?" its tone could make a viper blush.

"Y-yes," she said. Gil looked at her with shock.

"Lila, what are you doing! Don't talk to it!" he said.

The drake leaned forward, its head slithered through the air till it came eye to eye with Lila. Its void, hollow eyes stared deep within her.

"I thought I recognized that stench," it said, "I

remember your parents as part of the Keepers from the western coast. I was feeling rather generous that day, and sentenced them to life in the dungeon." It leaned back a bit. "Strike down the Lamb and I will release them!" Then it suddenly slinked in close again. "You do want to see your mommy and daddy again, *don't you?*"

Lila took a few small steps toward the drake, then turned to Gil and the Lamb.

"Lila, no!" called Rolldrin.

The Lamb squirmed in Gil's arms; he let it down. It started walking toward Lila; she slowly pulled her dagger. Gil stepped in front of the Lamb.

"Please, don't do this, Lila," said Gil.

"I'm sorry … I have to. I need my parents now more than ever," she said.

"You know he's lying! You have to know that!" shouted Gil.

"It's what I've always wanted, Gil …" she said.

"Yes," said the dragon, "do this simple task and I'll give you all you've ever hoped and dreamed for …"

The Lamb stepped around Gil, and strode up to Lila. It stared up at her with kind, sympathetic eyes, it seemed strangely calm.

"What a pitiful little thing!" said the drake, looming over her shoulder. "Kill it! Sacrifice it and claim your reward!"

"Lila, stop!" called Gil.

Tears streamed down her face as she looked into the Lamb's eyes. "I'm sorry … I'm so sorry …" She knelt down and stabbed the Lamb. Its corpse fell lifeless. She looked at her trembling, bloodied hands. "Wh-what have I done?"

The dragon withdrew its head, laughing and blowing flame into the air in its moment of triumph.

"At last!" the drake shouted. "Now nothing can stop me! All shall bow down and worship the great dragon, or be cleansed by dark fire! None will escape my wrath!"

Lila wept as she cradled the dead Lamb. She rocked back and forth saying, "I'm so sorry, I'm so sorry," over and over again. She placed the Lamb down and slowly stood up. Tears streamed down her face as she peered at the bloody dagger. With quivering hands, she slowly pointed it inward and placed the tip in front of her heart. She closed her eyes and started to lean forward. Suddenly, a large wet tongue lifted her backwards. She opens her eyes to see the Lion. It licked her again. She dropped the dagger and threw her arms around it and began to weep and laugh. The Lion nuzzled its face against hers.

"What is this *thing*?" the dragon asked confused. It brought its head in close to examine this very unexpected occurrence. "What kind of- …"

The Lion swiped the drake's face. It shrieked with pain then flew high into the sky. The Lion crouched, then sprung high into the air and caught the dragon's neck in its jaws. The Lion brought the drake down and cracked into its neck. It writhed and squirmed until a loud crunch resounded. The drake fell limp and lifeless in the jaws of the Great Lion. Soon, its corpse dissolved into nothingness.

The Lion came to Gil, it licked his face and rubbed its snout against him. Gil pet and cradled its head as he did when it was Lamb. Everyone gathered and celebrated their victory.

Shortly after, the Lion stood off by itself, then a bright archway of light appeared. Transparent people robed in white started to emerge from it. Men, women, young and old, came forth and mingled with the living.

The different men from Bejavia reunited with their wives and children. Velera stepped in from the doorway; Lila ran to meet her. She leapt into Velera giving her a big hug.

"Oh, my!" said Velera. "Good thing I'm a spirit now, otherwise you might have flattened me, hehe! I love you so very much, my dear Lila!"

"I've missed you, Nanna!" Lila said, now crying.

"I know, I know dear," said Velera, "you're a strong young woman, and … you'll make a great wife one day," she smiled and looked over Lila's shoulder at Gil. They approached the rest of the group.

"Everyone!" she started. "I'm supposed to tell you that all of you have been through so much together, savor these last goodbyes. Please, don't stay sad, for your futures are so bright. You have entered in to the age of the Lion, an age of salvation and prosperity. And, you'll need a new king to rule this renewed land, Gil!" she turned to Gil. "The Provider loves you, and is very proud of you. You and your family did what most would not. Although unsure at times, you stayed strong and kept the path He laid for you. And for all these reasons and more, He has anointed *you* king!"

At this the Lion put a paw on Gil's shoulder. He knelt down to it, and it breathed a crown of golden flame upon his head. After a moment, the crown took form. The fire was captured in gold; Velera then turned back to Lila.

"Young, Lila," she started, "your repenting heart has reached the Provider, and, if you couldn't tell by how the Lion's been kissing you, you have been forgiven under the blood of the Lamb," she said.

Several other figures came from the archway, including a sleek, beautiful, middle aged woman with dark, long flowing hair, and a stout, dark skinned man with a jolly face.

"Mom?" asked Bregal.

"Daddy!" squealed Mera.

"Hello, my little pearl bloom!" the stout man called. Mera lept into his arms, and he spun her around in the air. "Oh, it's so good to see you, my Maymera!"

The woman with the flowing hair approached Bregal.

"Bregal? You've grown so much, my sweet little boy," she said. Gently, she cradled his face in her hands, then kissed him on the forehead.

"Yeah … we sure missed you, mom …" Bregal said, while going to embrace her. Her tone turned solemn.

"I hope you can still remember how much I loved you both," she said. He kept her in his arms.

"Don't worry, mom. We knew," he smiled, tears trickled down his face. Then he jumped a little. "Mom, where's dad?" she smiled playfully.

"This must be my grandson!" she said, suddenly turning to Gil. The stout man turned to Gil as well.

"Yes, what a great young man too!" he said, wrapping his arms around him. "We've heard a lot about you!"

A rather young couple passed through the gate. A long, dark haired man and a short, blond haired woman, both with thin, elegant features watched Lila over Velera's shoulder. They held each other close as they stared lovingly till she noticed.

"Momma! Pappa!" Lila yelled, she raced over and jumped into their arms.

Several more joyous reunions occurred. Then, eventually, Velera got everyone's attention again.

"We love you all so much! But the time has come to go home. And on that note … Praise the

Provider! Praise the Lamb and the Lion! And long live King Gilgath!"

All shouted and rejoiced all the more! And so, the spirits said their goodbyes and returned through the arch of light. The Lion breathed on all who remained, then entered through the gate as well, off to lead the spirits to the Great Paradise.

Future

"And so, that's the story of how good defeated evil, small became great, and how perfect love saved us all. A nation was reborn, from dark to light, and the Knights of the Lamb were formed to maintain peace and justice throughout the land. That's the story of Gilgath and the Realm of the Drake."

With that, Mera closed the book. Three children sat on the floor at her feet. There were two boys and one girl. The girl lifted a hand.

"Granny, did all that really happen to you, grandpa, mommy, and daddy?" she asked.

Mera smiled softly. Her hair was now gray and her face had grown a bit wrinkled.

"Why, yes, dear, It seems like almost a lifetime ago, but it *did* happen. I felt it was time to finally tell you of some of our family's history. It only takes one person to change the world, after all, and you'll need to keep this in mind when it's *your* time to rule!"

"What about the cabin?" asked the younger boy.

"Well," Mera started, "me, grandpa and your dad lived there till we got the castle in order, then we all moved in here. But, your dad and mom used it to celebrate their marriage once … I think that was about three seasons before your older brother was born."

"But did mom *really* do it? Did she really *kill* the Lamb?" asked the older boy.

"Dear, you must understand," Mera began, "it had to happen. It had to be, so that way the Great Lion could be released, strike down the dark dragon, and lead the way to the Provider!" she paused for a moment. "Children, you may never fully understand all that has happened, but it was necessary to end the dark era. Now that we live in the era of the Lamb's blood, it's a new age, one of love, life and light. But young ones, you must decide what is important, and what to do with your time. For every choice you make further shapes this world. So I ask, who are you, and what will you do with *your* life in this world?"

About the Trinity Collections

Thank you so much for choosing to give this book a chance and supporting this mission! I hope it captivated you and touched your heart. You may have noticed, this is part of a "collection," most of my books fall into one of three collections, there's "With us," "For Us," and "In Us." Each collection is a different flavor from the Trinity. Not that they don't all make an appearance to an extent, but it's more of the subtle (or not so subtle) focal point. "For Us," focuses more on our loving heavenly father, our Abba, how He's rooting for us and makes things work for our good. "With us" are works focusing more on Jesus, His works, actions and journey and the people who He affected. "In Us," is more toward the Holy Spirit, how She's the never ending spring within, the Helper, these are more inward focused as well. All three are just another face to the same coin, so to speak. I hope and pray you get a chance to experience them all yourself, and get to taste Their sweetness, compassion, tenderness, and love, unconditional. Not just from these books, but in life! I hope you come to know Them all for yourself and in a way that's intimate and special to *you*.

Concept Art

note: If you pictured _anything_ differently in your head, that is perfectly fine. This is a collection that I made for the book. I hope you enjoy!

The Wyvern Totem

Far in the north, beyond Sky Dagger Mountain, a lone prisoner awaits his fate. Confined in a crude dimly lit cell deep in an icy cave, sits a bearded old man. He shivers on the cold floor.

"P-Provider, hear my plea," he starts, "I know it's been years, but I trust in your timing. Please, please warn my son of what's to come. Evil stirs in the north! Please, I beg of you, tell him before it's too late-" he was cut short.

A large, saber-toothed, lumbering, wooly, man-creature opened the cell and drug the man through to another section of the cave and tossed him on his face. The old man looked up to see a black wooden totem staring down at him. It's jutting, sharp features resembled a small, jagged dragon. Several other beast-like men surrounded him. The old man slowly stood up.

"You won't break me, Varcilyc! The food I live on can't spoil or be stolen!" he shouted at the totem.

"I don't need to, your capture and torment is sufficient for now," the totem's voice was deep and dark, yet somewhat faint.

"Your darkness is being severed from this world! Soon, there'll be nothing left!" the bearded man said.

"Oh, I assure you, as long as there's a desire for wrong, I will remain in this world," it said.

"The Lamb defeated you, your reign is over!" he said.

"Defeat? Maybe, I may be defeated, but I'm far from gone!" it said.

Dark essence flew from its eyes and seeped into the beast men. Their eyes turned black as they let out a raging roar.

Bregal gasped as he sprang up in bed. He was breathing franticly. Mera sat up too and placed a hand gently on his back.

"Breg? Are you alright?" she asked. Bregal jumped out of bed. He stared into the dark of the castle bedroom.

"I need to tell him!" he said.

"… Tell who?" she asked groggily.

"Gil! I need to tell Gil!" he said.

"About your nightmare?" she asked. He walked across the bedroom.

"The drake, it's-it's raising an army in the north!" he said.

"But it's dead, dear. The Lamb killed it years ago," she said.

"That's what I thought, but I heard it! And I saw-" he paused mid-reach for the door. "I saw dad."